The Wake
and
Bake Club

BENJAMIN PINE

Fulton Books
Meadville, PA

Published by Fulton Books 2022

ISBN 979-8-88505-510-9 (paperback)
ISBN 979-8-88505-511-6 (digital)

Printed in the United States of America

CHAPTER 1

Sleep seemed to linger mere seconds away. It was like trying to capture the wind with my bare hands. A zephyr caused the single chain of thoughts to rattle inside my skull. What was it that unnerved me, contemplating the first day of high school?

My grandmother had taught me to sleep with the covers pulled over my head. This safeguard would make it impossible for bad dreams to find me during the night. A small puddle of sweat dampened the sheets as I lay on my back. The bedding over my face was stifling. I threw them off and stood on the bed to reach the hanging chain of the ceiling fan. I watched the spinning blades of the fan for some time. The night continued at a slow pace.

This was a rare self-conscious moment in my life. Childhood had been that sweet time of innocence. In 1988, my family moved together in a ranch-style house with a pristine lawn. The suburbs of Delaware were the most mundane communities in the hemisphere.

No one in my neighborhood had ever been robbed or murdered. Accidental contacts were not viewed as intrusive. There was no technology tasked with making it unnecessary for one human being to ever ask anything of another. People felt safe without video cameras invading their privacy.

The time was just after four o'clock in the morning when I decided to make a bowl of cereal for breakfast. A car gunned along the street while I ate. It stopped near the driveway in front of my house. There was a loud *thwack* that echoed from outside. The sound came from the regular delivery of a bundle of newspapers hitting the sidewalk.

I got dressed in preparation for the brisk morning air. It was my job to deliver the morning and evening paper. The route wound through two neighborhoods: the Pencader Village and Four Seasons. I had to fold every paper, put a rubber band around each one, and place a paper on people's property.

I was encouraged by my parents to engage in many activities: Boy Scouts, art class, karate class, Little League baseball, and various other sports.

The most difficult task was collecting every payment for newspaper delivery. Everyone was never home at the same time. I resisted invitations to wait inside while the homeowner went to get the payment. There were unfamiliar odors inside other people's households. At times, older people kept me occupied with stories from their past.

Once, a family's German Shepherd had gotten loose and attacked. I ran off the front porch and across the lawn, but it did not take the enraged animal long to bring me down. The dog locked its sharp teeth around my calf muscle. Luckily, I had worn denim jeans. Loose coins and paper money flew out in every direction from a pouch tied around my waist.

The long walks during the early morning hours were pleasant. At least, when the weather was favorable. It was quiet, not a person in sight.

My family had awakened by the time I returned home. The smell of scrambled eggs with a side of bacon filled the air. I sat down with my father and younger brother at the dining room table. My father was teasing me about driving my brother to school on his first day. The thought made me chuckle. My dad's old work truck was always full of ladders, wires, and tools. He worked as an electrician at the University of Delaware.

"How about you? Do you want to ride in the old work truck?"

His attention turned to me. I declined, saying,

"I can walk from here."

The high school stood right across from Pencader Village. A ride on the school bus would take longer than walking. My mother was not fond of the idea, however.

"I don't want you crossing the highway during morning rush hour!" She yelled from the kitchen.

The conversation was interrupted by the irritating sound of the smoke detector. I tried to avoid eating some of my mother's meals. Something must have been wrong with my father's taste buds, though. "The char gives it that extra flavor," he would say.

I went to my bedroom after the business of clearing my sitting at the table. Then I gathered all of the school supplies and placed each item in my brand-new backpack.

Afterward, I sat on the edge of my bed. I stared into my closet, weighing the selection of new outfits to wear. My stomach began to churn. It felt like there was a brick lodged inside my stomach. I checked the bathroom down the hall. It was occupied. The weight of my body collapsed onto the comfortable mattress. My eyelids started to flicker.

"Benjamin Pine! Let's go!" My mother's voice cut through the quiet atmosphere in the house.

Reluctantly, I emerged from my room. A fog had crept across the landscape of my mind. My mother grabbed my bag lunch out of the refrigerator and dangled it in the air.

"Walk your brother to his bus stop," she instructed.

As we headed north, walking toward the front of the development, I noticed my clothes: they were old jeans and a long sleeve polo shirt—the same outfit worn to deliver papers earlier that morning. Regardless, we continued our journey. I inspected each house we passed along the way. They varied very little from one another. There were only two styles of buildings and four different colors of aluminum siding. I had noticed two or three houses in a row that were almost identical.

"Are you nervous, Ben?" My brother asked.

"Nah," I lied.

My mother's voice echoed inside my ears. Her incorporeal voice described the dangers of crossing Route 896 during rush hour. I envisioned speeding vehicles and my limp body bouncing off them like a pinball. Next, a mental picture of my funeral formed with intricate details. My weeping mother and grief-stricken father standing over a closed casket. Their firstborn son reduced to roadkill. In the end, I decided to take the bus to school.

First, I chaperoned Brandon to his bus stop. There was a small group of students my brother's age gathered at the corner. I studied their faces for any signs of nervousness. Then I gave Brandon a playful pat on his book bag and offered one last piece of advice.

"Just don't piss your pants. Everything else will take care of itself," I told him.

"Yeah," he scoffed.

I was the first high school student to arrive at the bus stop. There were two other students when the school bus approached the corner. We were the first to select seats on the bus. Of course, we chose to sit in the very last row of the seats. The only other boy sat uncomfortably close. I pressed against the cool metal side of the bus.

"Really?!" I hissed under my breath.

He adjusted his glasses with an index finger. I glanced at the blonde girl sitting across from us. She offered an indifferent shrug in response to the situation. The boy continued to face forward with a blank expression. I had never been acquainted with either of them. Brandon was my best friend. We spent every day growing up together.

The bus crawled through the neighborhood, left Pencader Village, and made multiple stops in Four Seasons. Many other students filled the empty seats. I maintained an interest on things outside the bus until a booming voice broke my concentration.

"Freshmen!?" An older boy growled.

No one else spoke a word. So I replied in a mousy tone.

"What?"

"It's a yes or no question, brain-dead. You are a freshman, aren't you?" he continued.

"You can smell fresh meat from a mile away," another boy announced.

A group of four older boys hovered in the aisle as the bus lurched forward. No one had ever spoken to me in such a manner. Especially in front of a large crowd.

"Find a seat!" The bus driver yelled.

"These are our seats," the first boy stated.

The young blonde girl was the first to relinquish her seat. I was last in the procession toward the front of the bus. There weren't many open seats on the bus. The group of boys threatened and impeded our progress.

"Don't let us find you in our seats again. You'll only get this one warning," one of them promised.

"It's a long school year. We can humiliate you five out of the seven days of the week," the first boy added.

I found the only available seat behind the bus driver. I was surrounded by students who were given labels like: nerd, geek, or lame. Students were excited to meet their teachers. The continued lurching movement of the bus and raw emotions caused an acid-like reflux from the pit of my stomach.

Finally, the bus parked in front of the high school. It was a long rectangular building made of red brick. The building reminded me of the factory. There were two entrances with dozens of concrete steps to climb. I passed through the central entry point of heavy glass doors. There was a large foyer with a staircase on the right to access the second floor. The principal's office was the first room in a long corridor on the left. I pressed onward through crowded halls to find my homeroom.

The first day of high school was filled with boring speeches and uninteresting syllabuses. I began nodding off during third period, earth science. The teacher's screaming voice brought me back to attentiveness. I noticed everyone was staring toward my location. The teacher directed me to stand at the back of the classroom as punishment.

Time was allotted for lunch after the fourth period class ended. There were four cafeterias to choose from. I found a seat in the nearest isolated corner. I refused to start a conversation with any other student.

The second half of the day was as dull as the first. I felt rejuvenated after the final bell rang and students were released. The number of cars traveling on the road separating the school and my neighborhood was very few. So I decided to walk home. I recalled as many cute girls as possible during the journey. I thought about the ones who were filling out more than others. I imagined which girl might want to accompany me at the first dance. Also, which girl would take my virginity.

I was the first to return home. I entered my bedroom and picked up the TV remote. Suddenly, my insides felt like they were going to force their way out. I made a mad dash to the bathroom. My bowels exploded and sputtered into the toilet. Water splashed upward, soaking my backside. An audible sigh escaped from my lips.

My brother was the second to arrive. We watched cartoons and discussed various opinions of our day. I told stories to Brandon about my experience at his middle school—I was curious about "Mr. Vasso the Fatso" being principal, still.

Later, we took turns describing our day to our parents.

It was the major topic of discussion during dinner. Our parents acted very interested to hear every detail, and their eagerness caused a slight feeling of embarrassment. My parents had an even greater tendency to dote over my brother.

The second day of school was more of the same routine. I started by folding each morning paper and wrapping it with a rubber band. Then I made a trek through the neighborhoods, tossing papers whenever necessary. Afterward, I ate breakfast with my family and walked with Brandon to his bus stop.

I rode the bus to Glasgow. The last row of seats remained empty. I sat in the second to the last row. It was a deliberate effort to make my presence known to the older boys. They each gave me a knowing glance as they took their seats.

I walked home after school again. The straps of my book bag dug into my shoulders due to the weight of the new textbooks. Later, my mother covered the books with brown paper bags from the supermarket. My father drove me to a karate class on Tuesday and Thursday night. He was good-natured about driving me back and forth, even though I hadn't made much progress in the class. I was still a white belt after training for two years. A white belt was the first one given to students. The instructor required the class to meditate for long periods of time.

Sometimes, my father would wait for a conversation to start. Then he would start the engine and drive. This evening, he turned to me after the session was over.

"You have a crush on any of the girls at school?" He began.

"No," I answered. I felt my cheeks start to burn.

"Don't take too long, or the upperclassman will scoop up all the pretty girls," he continued.

"I have plenty of time," I assured him.

"You know…I was only seventeen when I married your mother. My parents had to sign papers for me to get married," he explained.

He had told this same story on innumerable other occasions. I had begun to feel some responsibility. There were fewer than nine months between my birthday and their wedding. I had done the math.

CHAPTER 2

The very next day, I stood at the threshold to one of the cafeterias at school. The room was very large and crowded. I scanned the scene, searching for an open seat, so I could enjoy my brown bag lunch. My eyes darted in a zigzag direction. The endeavor was interrupted, when I glimpsed a familiar face.

It felt as though fate had struck me in the face. My consciousness was propelled into an unusual state of sensory. I had been reduced to an observer-participant in relation to my own existence. A consolidated memory flashed before my mind's eye. I was a young child in kindergarten. A youthful girl led me by the hand toward the middle of the gym floor. Then matters took an unexpected turn.

Suddenly, we were blindsided by another girl. She scrambled to separate us.

"That's my boyfriend!" She cried.

A teacher had witnessed the entire incident unfold. She intervened and dragged the disgruntled girl away. The tormented look on the girl's face was haunting. Her temper flared and her raven tresses swayed. My gaze kept returning to her eyes though. Those eyes burned with white-hot intensity.

Those eyes! Even now, they caused a shiver to race down my spine. My scrutiny had not gone unnoticed; our eyes had locked. It felt like my soul was being dissected. The discovery of this childhood acquaintance left my thoughts in a disjointed conundrum.

My extreme astonishment was interrupted by the loud activity in the crowded area. I turned and began to walk away. Others may have been alarmed as my pace quickened. At length, I ran in fear of being pursued. I left the building through an exit leading to the student parking lot, stopping to lean against the rear wall.

Without warning, another memory brought me back to the summer after kindergarten. It was a day spent at the water park with my family. My parents rested on a couple of lounge chairs as I played in a giant wave pool. The water was calm and refreshing. It felt comfortable wading deeper into the crowded pool.

"Stay where I can see you, Ben," my mother warned.

At first, I was heedful of her warning. The distance to my parents was no greater than a few yards. I eased through the crowded pool with caution. The other swimmers weren't as polite. I grew tired of having my space invaded. The only open path of water was near the back wall. So I swam to the far end of the wave pool.

Suddenly, the water began to churn. The back wall came alive with activity. The change of position created a current that pulled me beneath the surface. Then a pause in the motion allowed me to emerge from the water. The wall returned to its original position. This movement displaced a miniature tsunami of chlorinated water that slapped me in the face.

The speed of the mechanism increased. Tidal wave after tidal wave was created. The powerful flow of the water became overwhelming. I started to drown in the deep water, struggling underneath dozens of oblivious swimmers. My field of vision began to narrow. I made a frantic attempt to reach the floor of the pool. The turbulent water negated every effort. My whole body convulsed, water gushed into my mouth, and my eyes closed.

Finally, a bolt of excitement tingled my senses. I felt the hard surface of the bottom scrape against my foot. Self-preservation gave me the strength to propel myself upward. I launched out of the water between a mother holding her young daughter. The crown of my head struck the girl's chin.

The mother swam to the side of the pool clutching her daughter in one arm. She lifted her daughter to safety. Then she returned to aid in my safe removal also.

I noticed the young girl studying my face with concern. The sudden recognition of this girl staring in such a grave manner caused embarrassment. It was the same raven-haired girl from kindergarten. The girl leaned close and kissed my lips.

"He's hurt!" She cried.

I must have bitten down on my lip during the collision. I felt blood trickle down my chin and wiped it away with my forearm.

Her mother wasn't as concerned about my well-being. Actually, she was quite livid.

"You could apologize! You little weirdo!" She yelled.

Right then, I vomited chlorinated water. Without warning or explanation, I ran away.

I didn't dare loiter outside the building any longer. My next impulse was to hide in the one place she wasn't permitted. I set out to find the nearest men's room. For the next few moments, I roamed the halls. The possibility of transferring to a different school occupied my mind.

The bathroom was empty. I scanned for any stalls containing people. Then I tossed my uneaten lunch in the trash. My head felt like an overheated radiator. My memories scintillated like flashbacks from a bad acid trip. I splashed cold water from a sink on my face. An instant later, my eyes searched the mirror on the wall for my reflection.

Instead, there was the sinister countenance of the person whom I met in the cafeteria. It had been transformed into a hellish landscape. The charred remains of students littered the area around her. She was a goth succubus. Black Cupid's bow lips curved into an inhuman grin, revealing fangs that rivaled porcelain. She didn't bother to conceal her disgust. The look she gave me said, "Yes, I hate you. I hate the world."

A group of rowdy teenage boys came crashing through the doorway. I was startled by the door slamming against the wall. The mirror allowed me to observe the students enter. Two of the teens were familiar. Their family names leaped into my head: Woodall and Vitale. They lived along my paper route in Four Seasons.

Woodall lit a cigarette. Then he looked into the mirror, and our eyes locked for a split second.

"What?!" He snapped.

I moved toward the exit with caution. The group had positioned themselves in a manner that blocked my progress. Still, I continued to step onward. My hesitation allowed Woodall enough time to recognize me too.

"Hey, I know who you are. This lame ass comes to my house begging for money. What are you doing standing around in the men's room?" said Woodall.

"No. I was leaving," I stated.

Woodall stretched the arm holding the burning cigarette in my direction.

"Here. Hold this for me, lame," he commanded.

Another teen tried to snatch the cigarette. Woodall slapped the reaching hand down with precision. I obeyed the order with urgency in my movements.

"You were lurking in here." Woodall yelled over the sound of his urine splashing in the stall toilet.

Suddenly, the men's room door collided with the wall. An older man hurried around the corner. He plucked the burning cigarette from my grasp. Then he placed it under the sink faucet to extinguish the ember.

"Are you having a smoke break?" The man asked.

"Just using the restroom, sir."

Woodall's voice rang out from the stall.

The others all chimed in with total agreement. I was too stunned by the turn of events to speak.

"Get out of here then. I'll remember your faces," the man stated.

He stood and stared into my eyes. I was frozen in place. The others scattered out of the cramped room.

"You come with me," the man instructed.

The unfamiliar faculty member escorted me to the principal's office. I felt like a prisoner being thrown inside a jail cell. He left me alone in the office. I overheard fragments of his conversation with the secretary outside. He inquired about the availability of the principal. Also, he insisted the office aid find a container for the soggy cigarette. Then the conversation continued in low murmurs.

My solitude allowed me time for reflection. I reminisced about the ethereal figure from my childhood again. She had full-bodied, blue-black hair that resembled a puddle of crude oil. Every color in the spectrum shimmered as light reflected off each strand. She had Mediterranean features. Her nose was delicate, though the nostrils flared with intensity. Her chin molded with exacting detail. There was a luxurious smoothness to her skin.

I had accumulated enough courage to approach her at the beginning of the first grade. The encounter during the summer break had enkindled something inside me. My face filled with warmth as we spoke.

"Your mom saved my life," I told her.

"My name is Toni," she replied.

The bell rang to signal the end of lunch. I snapped back to the reality of my current situation. The halls grew quiet as students evacuated. I felt restless sitting alone in the office.

Soon, I became aware of the principal's arrival. An indistinguishable conversation took place outside the office. Then the principal entered his office and introduced himself.

"Hello, I'm Mr. Cosgrove," he said.

His voice was booming and filled the room. He strutted toward his desk with an air of importance. His suit was neat and crisp. He sat in a glistening leather chair and held up the envelope with the cigarette inside.

"Disgusting habit," he stated.

The evidence was discarded into the trash.

"It is too early in the school year for this nonsense," he continued.

There was an awkward pause as he studied my demeanor.

"Was it a game of hot potato and you got burnt?" He inquired.

"Something like that," I replied.

"I'm more concerned about your health than anything else. You are much too young to start smoking."

"I don't really…" I muttered.

"Next time, I'll have you cleaning bathrooms for a week."

He raised an arm and conducted me out of his office. I was not prepared for this abrupt dismissal.

"Be careful of the company you keep, Mr. Pine."

I gave the principal a backward glance over my left shoulder. The manner in which he spoke my name caused a momentary halt in forward movement. Most of his remarks felt unanswerable. Then I found my way to class without delay or hesitation.

CHAPTER 3

I have never openly stated my intellect to be superior than any other. It must be remembered that most teenagers believe they know everything. My own folly was daydreaming about girls during class. This must account for my abhorrent academic achievements.

Eventually, the first report card arrived in the mail. There was a miserable silence as my parents studied the official slip of paper. A childish wish entered my mind. I should have delayed the delivery or torn the report card to pieces and thrown it away.

My father diverted his attention away from the report card first. His eyes were intense as he peered in my direction. My jaw stiffened and I ground my teeth. He left my mother's side and closed the distance between us. His stride was long and quick. He charged down the hall until he disappeared. Sounds coming from my bedroom were hard to gauge. I turned toward the disturbance.

My mother hampered my movement by pulling my hair. She grabbed a fistful of hair and shook my head back and forth. She expressed her disappointment and shoved the report card in front of my face. Her conduct caused me to wince in fear. Later, I sulked in my room and studied the damage extenuated by my father. He had toppled furniture. The cable connected to the TV had been ripped out of the wall. I went a couple of weeks without TV.

Otherwise, there was very little change in my routine. I was still able to partake in all the extracurricular activities,. I continued to deliver my morning and evening papers. I would disappear for hours using the excuse of collecting payments. My parents did not accept excuses when it was time to study, however. It was mandatory for me to be observed studying at the dining room table. I was required to present completed homework assignments. There were no signs of leniency as the holiday season approached.

Christmas morning, I pretended to be asleep while Brandon crept into my bedroom. He threw himself on my bed. Then he jumped up and down. I goaded him to do the same to our parents. Afterward, he returned and pulled me out to the living room by my arm.

The living room resembled a scene from a Norman Rockwell painting. There was a gentle snowfall outside. An unblemished blanket of white covered the ground. There were four Christmas stockings hung on the mantle over the fireplace. They were brimming with toys and various candies. A large pine tree was the focal point. Lights, tinsel, and a variety of ornaments adorned its branches. A large golden star emitted a warm glow from the top of the tree. The huge pile of gifts encroached upon the room.

My father came into the room and sat on the couch. My mother made hot cocoa for the family. They both wore fluffy cotton robes. Everyone sipped cocoa and took turns opening presents.

"Which one is your favorite?" My father asked.

"We're not done yet. We have to see what Santa left at your grandparents' house," my mother interrupted.

"Are we going to have time to visit both?" My brother inquired.

"We should have enough time," my father assured him.

Afterward, my mother prepared a huge breakfast. Smoke billowed out of the kitchen. I had removed the batteries from the smoke detector, previously. I feared a lack of breathable air. So I rushed into the kitchen and prepared a bowl of cereal.

"Not hungry?" my mother asked.

"I'm saving room for Christmas dinner," I explained.

I returned to the dining room table to eat, pausing to offer a silent prayer for my grandmother's cooking. Her holiday meals included a delicious golden-brown turkey with all the trimmings. The homemade desserts were out of this world. A tear formed in the corner of my eye. It could have been the reminiscent thoughts, or it could have been the smoke streaming from the kitchen.

"Can I wear one of my new outfits?" I asked.

"Me too?" My brother added.

Brandon and I sat in the living room after we had finished eating breakfast. We chose new clothes to wear during our holiday visits. Then we played with our new toys. *Life couldn't get much better*, I thought.

My parents were preparing for the holiday visits in the hallway bathroom. The sound of running water from the shower could be heard in the living room. Voices from the bathroom were muted by the splash of the water. All of a sudden, an outburst from my mother was audible. She used foul language that caused me to cringe.

A loud crackling sound made my heart skip a beat. The lights on the Christmas tree flickered. I heard a loud *thud*. Then the bathroom door burst open. I ran into the dining room and peered down the hall. My father's naked body was shrouded by the shower curtain. He locked himself inside the master bedroom. My mother followed in close pursuit. She screamed more obscenities and attempted to bang the locked door down.

"What is happening?" I cried.

"Go back in the living room with Brandon!" She screamed.

My father had dialed 911 as soon as he was safe. It didn't take long for the police to arrive. I saw the lights flashing as they positioned vehicles along the street. I expected to hear a knock on the front door. Instead, the police broke down the door in full riot gear. Police take domestic violence very seriously. I'm sure they don't want to work on Christmas morning, either.

Officers signaled for Brandon and I to remain in one area of the living room. Then they traversed the house with caution. My mother was confronted by the two lead officers holding shields. She charged straightaway. The two officers pinned my mother against the wall with their shields. It required a concerted effort to quell her.

The officers were kept off-balance by her animated thrashing. She managed to lock onto one officer with her teeth. She pushed another officer's shield upward and he stumbled back. Then she threw her entire body against the second shield. The rest of the squad pounced on her like a group of linebackers.

Eventually, the officers were able to gain the upper hand. Her hands were cuffed and her ankles were shackled to prevent kicking. She cursed the officers as the ungainly group exited.

After the all clear was given, paramedics entered through the broken doorway. They urged my father to open the locked door. He was placed on a gurney and brought to an ambulance. I followed the procession to the ambulance. And then I watched everyone vanish.

I stood outside on the front lawn in shock. The events were hard to believe, and they happened so fast. The police never took a statement. Nobody asked, "Are you okay?" No one spoke a word to me or my brother. I was delighted by the calm in the air after everyone had left.

Brandon and I spent the day putting the house in order. We took our presents to our rooms, threw away the gift wrappers, and straightened the furniture. Later, I made grilled cheese sandwiches for us to eat.

My father was held overnight at the hospital. He was the first to return. He gathered some vital belongings and packed them into his truck. He gave my brother a hug and shook my hand.

"Your mother will be home soon. I don't want to be here when that happens," he explained.

Two days later, my mother was released from custody. Her father drove from Pennsylvania to post bail. Upon arrival, she described her ordeal. She was filled with rage and bitter hatred for my father. His intention was to file for divorce.

The whole reason behind the chaos on Christmas eluded me for years. I learned the truth from my father. The guilt of infidelity had caught up with him. So he had revealed this plan to leave my mother for another woman.

The revelation caused my mother to lose her self-control. She had thrown a hair dryer into the shower with my father. Luckily, he was an electrician. He had made certain to install GFI outlets throughout the entire house. The surge of power had caused the ground wire to trigger an interruption in the flow of electricity. Still, my father had been delivered a slight jolt. His knees buckled and he fell out of the shower. He was treated for minor burns on his feet.

"I don't know why I chose that exact moment. Sometimes, things seem too perfect. Some people feel the need to sabotage themselves," he explained.

CHAPTER 4

After a lapse of some days spent at home in idleness, I was delighted to be back to school. The solace was short-lived, however. I lost interest in most things. I no longer felt the desire to participate in any extracurricular activities. No one offered to take me, regardless.

There was a new student in many of my classes. Her name was Ashley Hayes. She transferred from Caravel Academy. The academy was considered a prestigious school for privileged individuals. News of her arrival traveled fast throughout the school. I jumped at any opportunity to accompany her, or carry her books, or share my lunch, etc.

She was recruited by the cheerleading squad straightaway. I attended every home game to watch her cheer.

One day, Ashley and I were having lunch together. The table was crowded with other students vying for her attention. I was close enough to hear her conversation anyway. She was talking with another student about the lack of fireworks at football games.

"We should ask someone on the student council to bring it up at one of the meetings," she suggested.

Meanwhile, I took it upon myself to procure pyrotechnics. The sale of fireworks was illegal. It was another example of how mediocre it was living in Delaware. The mission to obtain fireworks was a failure. I was able to find a flare pistol, though.

My father made many new purchases after leaving my mother. The signal flares and pistol were on his new boat. I smuggled the stolen pistol and five flares to a Glasgow High football game. I lurked in the shadows outside the fence, wearing dark winter clothes and a thick scarf to cover my face. The Glascow Dragons won the game 45 to 24.

I shot three flares into the night sky when the final score was announced. Faculty members found my location as soon as the third flare reached its apex. There were police officers at the game for security, also. They trudged along with their hands on their weapons. The angry mob of adults chased me away from the football field.

At first, I ran through an open field with no place to hide. I loaded the flare gun during my flight. Then I fired into the middle of the mob. Some individuals dove to the ground, while others stopped their pursuit.

There was no place to elude capture. So I darted toward a nearby neighborhood. A parked vehicle provided a place to hide. The dull yellow light emitted from the streetlamps fell here and there. I snaked through the dark areas, using hedges along the residential streets to escape.

A school-wide search was initiated to find the guilty culprit. That didn't stop people from taking credit. I considered giving Ashley some subtle hint it was me. I spent Monday morning trying to make up my mind.

At lunch, I heard Ashley giving her own recount of the mayhem. She spoke about police canvassing the neighborhood for hours. Patrol cars barricaded every corner and people came out of their homes.

"It was insane! Total chaos! The flares started small fires on the ground," she said.

"They'll never let us have fireworks now," someone interjected.

"I think this was even better—it was bananas!" She replied.

"You really enjoyed it?" I asked.

"Really. I've never seen so much excitement," she insisted.

I made a discreet motion for Ashley to leave the cafeteria. She stared and waited for me to say something to explain.

"You have to see this!" I urged.

She accompanied me through crowded halls until we stood in front of my locker. I spun the dial and gained entry.

She noticed the bright orange pistol inside my locker. She grabbed the pistol and studied it with intensity. I had no chance of stopping her.

"Hey, don't take it out!" I scolded.

I took possession of the flare gun. There was an inadvertent touch of our hands. I realized how close we stood. The flare gun was tossed inside my locker with an indifference.

"You did this for me?" She inquired.

I nodded my head to confirm her suspicion. The affirmation earned her home phone number. She wrote the digits on my palm. Then she walked away with a light bouncing step. I followed her with my eyes until she disappeared around a corner.

Later that day, classes were interrupted by a fire alarm. Everyone evacuated the building in a long procession.

An unshakable grip seized my arm. A faculty member yanked me from the crowd outside. I was escorted to the principal's office with the vicelike grip maintained around my arm. A peculiar sensation raised the hair on the back of my neck. The circumstances in connection with the fire alarm were about to become clear.

The contents of my locker smoldered in a pile on the floor of the principal's office. The principal picked up a piece of melted, orange plastic. He held it between his index finger and thumb.

"Are you able to recognize this debris?" He inquired.

Mr. Cosgrove paused to allow a response. I decided it was better to keep the conversation minimal.

"Do you have anything to say for yourself?" He continued.

Mr. Cosgrove conveyed a seriousness in all that he said. I knew my actions were beyond any defense. The stillness was so profound o ne might have heard a pin drop.

"I'll accept whatever comes next, sir," I answered.

"I was young once, believe it or not. I have learned patience over the years. And I don't believe in suspension. You will reimburse the school for damages. Also, you will show up for detention on Saturday morning. Every Saturday, in fact, until I feel you have learned a lesson. Now, get out of my sight. Before you test my patience any further, Mr. Pine."

There were some familiar faces in detention. Woodall and Vital, two of the bathroom smokers, were seated at one of the long tables in the library. Toni stood near a large desk in the corner. I derived no pleasure from this extraordinary coincidence.

"You look lost, lame. This isn't the chess club meeting," Woodall announced.

Ashley was the next person to enter the library. Everyone followed her movements with intense scrutiny. She sat in a chair next to me, and I didn't have the nerve to breathe a word to her. Her smile and cheerfulness were encouragement, however.

"Why haven't you called?" She whispered.

"Are you two boyfriend and girlfriend?" Woodall asked in an obnoxious tone.

Mr. Cosgrove entered and allowed the heavy door to slam behind him. He took a seat behind the large desk. Then he handed some items to Toni.

"Hand these out to the others, please," he instructed her.

She began to pass out paper and pencils to the students serving detention. Her outfit differed from the gothic attire worn during normal school hours. Instead, she wore a black sweater and a black dress with a colorful floral print. Her makeup was subtle, natural tones, except for the smoky effect around her eyes.

She slid a piece of paper in front of me on the table. Then she stabbed the pencil downward on the tabletop.

The point of the pencil exploded into tiny shards. The pencil she deposited on the table was useless.

"What is your malfunction, psycho?" Ashley asked.

"I would like an essay describing how you envision yourself in this world. It needs to be a thousand words or more—different words from your friends, Mr. Woodall. Don't mess with the bull." Mr. Cosgrove explained.

Ashley scribbled a brief message on her paper. *Write mine, please,* it read. I shook my head side to side, signaling my objection. She replaced my broken pencil with her pencil. I felt her free hand slide up my inner thigh and squeeze. The essay for Ashley was finished before detention ended.

Mr. Cosgrove remained inside the library. He sat at the desk reading the entire time. Toni was directed to carry out any task he required. I avoided any other direct eye contact with her.

Detention ended after two hours had elapsed. I had only finished writing half of my own essay. Mr. Cosgrove dismissed the students.

"Mr. Pine…Mr. Woodall. I expect you gentlemen to report for detention next week," he stated.

Ashley was waiting for me in the hallway. She gripped both of my hands and swung them in a playful manner.

"Thank you, Ben," she said.

"I'm not sure if it makes much sense," I told her.

"I'm sure it was great. He probably doesn't even read them. But more importantly, I thought you would have called me by now."

"Just busy, ya know."

"Do you want a ride home?"

As we spoke, I noticed each person exit the library. They all glanced in my direction. I sensed their expressions questioning why someone like Ashley would be having a conversation with someone like me. Toni's nasty sideway glance bothered me the most.

"Doesn't she have anything better to do with her time?" I muttered.

"Who? Wednesday Addams?" Ashley joked.

"Yeah… I appreciate the offer. But I have to go visit my dad. It's a whole thing. A really complicated thing." I explained.

CHAPTER 5

At first, my father disappeared. I had very little contact with him after he left. The main impediment was my mother's behavior. She had fully committed to making the divorce a difficult process, and even a civil conversation between the two adults became impossible.

It occurred to me that I might be able to persuade my mother's opinion. I waited until she wasn't in such a terrible mood. Then I explained that visitation with my father was inevitable. She didn't agree right away.

Eventually, she was prepared to allow a visit. My father postponed the visit, however. He wanted to keep his location a secret. Also, he wanted the introduction of his new girlfriend to be perfect.

Stacy was present during the first visit. I had no idea how long my father had been in a relationship with her. She was a twenty-three-year-old student at the University of Delaware. She acted younger than her age at times. They had moved into a large two-story house together.

My father ensured Brandon and I did not learn the location of the house. First, he drove in a misleading direction. Then he stopped at multiple locations, indicating the need for: food, gas, or various other items. Finally, he provided blindfolds before we arrived.

Brandon and I had our own bedrooms. The rooms were fully furnished down to the smallest detail. The entire house was decorated with brand-new items.

We visited my father every other Saturday. Sometimes, he took us to eat at a restaurant. He always offered to keep us overnight, but I felt more comfortable in my old bed. Besides, my mother was always anxious for our return. She asked where my father lived after every visit.

One particular Saturday my mother was poised for a confrontation. I had walked home from detention and parked myself in front of the TV. My mother kept finding reasons to enter my room and ask questions.

"Is that what you're wearing?" She began.

"Yeah," I replied.

"I hope it won't be too cold. What does he have planned?"

"I don't know."

"Is she going to be there?"

"I guess."

My mother placed some clean clothes inside my dresser drawer. Then she stormed out of the room. She returned after a few minutes and hovered by the doorway.

"Why won't you tell me where your father lives?" She continued.

"He makes us wear a blindfold," I told her.

"You let him blindfold you every time?"

"Yeah."

Her interrogation was interrupted by the sound of a vehicle in the driveway. My father stayed inside his truck. He gave the horn a quick tap. The noise alerted my mother. She hurried outside to confront my father. Brandon and I followed her.

She launched into a fervent verbal attack. My father ignored her rant. She made an attempt to open the driver's side door. It was locked. So, she stomped around to the passenger door. That proved to be futile, also. She began to beat on the window. I was afraid the glass might shatter.

My father pleaded for her to calm down from the secure cab of his truck. Then he started to back his truck out of the driveway. She followed the slow progress of the vehicle. The situation began to escalate. I became worried for my mother's safety.

She stepped in front of the truck as my father straightened out the vehicle onto the street. He drove toward her at a very slow rate of speed. The truck came into contact with her. She was forced to yield and allowed the truck to pass. Next, she latched onto the bed of the truck. My father increased the speed of the truck. My mother was not able to maintain pace with the fast-moving vehicle. Her shoes dragged along the pavement. The truck careened around the first corner, and my mother lost her grip. She rolled on the street for a few yards. Afterward, she collected herself and made note of her wounds.

Brandon and I disappeared before my mother discovered us watching her. We retreated to my bedroom. There was no escape, however. My mother's aggravated state caused me to be concerned. I thought I knew what would happen.

My mother stormed into the master bedroom. Then she came into my room, wielding one of my father's abandoned belts. She held it high, ready to strike. She charged toward me with a wild look in her eyes. Now I had become the focus of her anger.

The belt leather stung my face. Not hard enough to leave a mark, but it stung. It hurt in more ways than one.

"You are not going to keep secrets from me!" She screamed.

My eye throbbed inside its socket. Still, I was able to see the belt rise and fall. The blow struck my chest. My mother was prepared to continue her assault. Brandon wanted to intervene. I pushed him back with my outstretched hand, however.

"Where does your father live?" She yelled.

"I can't tell you," I answered.

"You're just like him. You're a lying bastard, just like your father!" She screeched.

She slung the belt, and I was struck several more times. The blows came in swift repetition. Nothing was held back. Brandon watched with a sickened look on his face. I fell to the floor and curled into a ball. An unexpected pain radiated from the back of my head. My mother had turned the belt and hit me with the metal buckle. The following blows made a loud *thump* on my back. I was beaten like a drum by the weight of the buckle.

As sudden as the beating had started, it stopped when my mother left the room. Brandon crouched down next to me on the floor. I convulsed as uncontrollable sobs left my body. There, on the floor, I suffered for many minutes.

At length, I contacted my father by phone and described the attack. He offered to call the authorities. We agreed to meet without my mother's knowledge. He brought a camera to document my injuries. I declined his request to pose and have my picture taken. I suspect that he wanted to use the photos in court.

"You're welcome to come live with me," he offered.

I decided to remain at my childhood home, though. There was no custody agreement. My mother was refusing to sign divorce papers. In the end, my brother was the one to move. My mother was heartbroken the day Brandon left. She urged me to leave with him.

My mother became a different person. She no longer lamented the loss of her beloved husband. Wild parties were thrown at the house. They were an ongoing celebration of my parents' separation. She would introduce a new boyfriend every few days.

One day, she brought home a motorcycle club member. My childhood home in suburbia became a den for a motorcycle club and random thugs. Tattoos of flowers and butterflies appeared on my mother. She talked nonstop about buying her own motorcycle.

I was lured into the middle of the chaos: drugs, alcohol, loud music, and scantily dressed women. People indulged their wildest fantasies as I sat at the dining room table. It was difficult to dismiss my overwhelmed feelings. I searched the premises for my mother. My attention was diverted to a growing crisis.

Suddenly, an argument took a sudden turn to violence. The fight proceeded inside a circle of motorcycle club members. I gazed at the crowd in the living room with emotions of wonder and horror. The people I observed were: whooping and yelling, spilling drinks, flickering ashes anywhere, breaking items, and worse.

A mountain of a man sat down opposite of my position at the table. He wore a leather vest with an identical patch as the other bikers. I toyed with a cigarette I had stolen. There was a pilfered red solo cup full of beer, also. He leaned closer and pointed to the cigarette in my hand.

"Do you smoke?" He bellowed over the noise.

"Not without a lighter," I yelled.

"What do you like to be called?"

"Ben."

"You can call me Weedeater."

He stood and walked away from the table. I watched as he searched for items in the kitchen. He returned from his scavenger hunt with: a lighter, an ashtray, a pen, and a scrap of paper. Then he produced a sandwich bag full of green leafy nuggets. My apprehension was difficult to conceal. He separated seeds and stems from the dried leaves. He ate the stems and seeds. His name made sense now.

He broke down the remaining nuggets into fine leavings. A joint was rolled with a pack of papers taken from his vest. He wrote something down as the joint hung from his lips. Then he folded the paper into an envelope and scraped the rest of the weed inside.

Weedeater had a Cheshire cat-sized grin on his face as he smoked the joint. The sweet aroma was intoxicating. I felt the wild influences infecting me, and a tremor assaulted my frame. An electrifying wave of activity coursed up and down my spine.

Weedeater did not suffer an ethical dilemma. He placed the joint inside the ashtray and pushed them across the table. He slid the package toward me too. I didn't understand his departing words. I was too busy coughing from my first inhalation of smoke.

There was no profound revelation forthcoming. The narcotic in my system didn't make me feel any different. I felt the same melancholy, watching other people have fun and feel at home. The scene brought to mind images from the children's book, *Where the Wild Things Are.*

So I gathered the items on the table: the lighter, the cigarette, the pouch of weed, the cup of beer, and the ashtray with the roached joint. I carried the items to my room and set them down on my dresser. I took a sip of warm beer. The taste was disgusting. My room appeared untouched by the rowdy mob. There was a noticeable decrease in noise after the door was closed.

In the next instant, I heard my mother being initiated by motorcycle club members in the master bedroom. I put on some music to drown out the obscene sounds coming from my mother's room. It was a struggle to sleep. I sank little by little into slumber. My dreams harassed me with innumerable images of desolation.

I bolted upright after an indefinite short period. My sleep was disturbed by the mass exodus of bikers. Motorcycle engines roared down the street. The sheer number rattled windows as they rode away.

It was a brisk Saturday morning in February, and the routine was the same. I ate a bowl of cereal for breakfast. The newspapers were prepared for delivery. Then they were tossed throughout the neighborhoods. I completed another ridiculous essay in detention. The rest of the day was spent alone in my room.

I smoked the roached-out joint from the previous night, watched cartoons on TV, and dumped out the packet of weed. There was a phone number and a brief message on the inside.

"Call if you need anything."

My second experimentation with marijuana was very different. The drug created a feeling of euphoria, at first.

The feeling became an out-of-body experience. A gentle pull lifted me above my physical self.

Suddenly, I had the well-known feeling that someone else was there. I spun around to catch the lurking figure. The other figure mimicked my posture and movement. I lost awareness of who the original was and who the double was.

I became obsessed with the idea that the other would become a constant companion.

"You're never going to graduate," said the shade.

My shadow wanted me to know his affect. He had control over me, and there was nowhere to hide.

"Don't you want to attend classes at the university? Do you think they'll accept an idiot who had to repeat a year?"

"That won't happen," I mumbled.

"You could get a GED. A Government Equivalent of a Dumbass."

I was consumed by a deep feeling of bewilderment. I came crashing back down to earth, back down into my body with a start. The pile of weed vanished at a quick rate. I smoked more and more to regain that feeling of euphoria. Finally, I called the number Weedeater had left.

"The stuff you gave me is gone," I told him.

"No problem. I can stop by shortly."

CHAPTER 6

The next morning, I decided to ride public transportation downtown. The bus to downtown Newark stopped along Route 896 in front of my development. The public library was my final destination. Newark Library was built with red brick, much like Glascow High. I entered through a set of large glass doors.

A pungent odor from the decaying books punched me in the face. The smell reminded me of cinnamon. People spoke in hushed tones. A melodic voice carried throughout the cool, thickly-scented air. I was drawn to find the source. The voice originated in the children's literature section. I walked to the right of the main desk, following the raspy tone.

Toni Shay Marciano was reading Dr. Seuss to a group of young children. She gave a slight pause as I came into view. The children took notice of my arrival also. Toni had to find her place in the book again.

I would not allow our chance encounter deter me from my goal. I scoured rows of books for material that might aid my education. Also, I selected a few magazines from the periodical section, including a classic car magazine and Popular Science. Next, I took a seat at one of many large tables with brass lamps attached at the center. The arrangement of books and magazines occupied a large area on the table.

The reading material kept me preoccupied for a while. I found some books worthwhile to check out of the library. My attention was diverted to a dark figure standing in the middle of the library.

Toni had affixed herself in my line of sight. There was a menacing grin on her face. She proceeded to saunter toward the exit, pausing at the large glass door. A glance was given to make certain my attention was held captive. Then she shook her breasts in my direction and gave the door one violent shove.

I remained at the library for the majority of the day. A great deal of time was spent in the audio-visual room watching *Citizen Kane*. I was surprised by the variety of entertainment at the library. There were TV sets and VHS tapes for reviewing. Also, there were records and cassette tapes for listening.

Monday, I returned to school. I was sober. I did not want to have an attack of paranoia. One day without an incident would have been ideal. Instead, Ashley waited in front of my locker. She gave the impression of being standoffish.

"Why does it feel like you're mad?" I asked.

"Emily told me that Tina heard someone say that we had sex. The word 'slut' was scrawled across my locker!" She shouted.

"I didn't do it. I'd never start a rumor about you."

"It doesn't matter. This still has to happen," she whispered.

I gave her a puzzled look. She caught me by surprise with a hard slap to my face. Then her index finger was pointed at my face. She raised her voice, allowing the crowd to hear it.

"Don't talk to me…ever! You rotten bastard liar!"

Students had conversations about the scene as suspicion swirled throughout school. I wanted to put an end to the rumors, but the stronger my denial, the more people believed. I received congratulatory pats on the back from the older boys in the back row of the bus. I was alienated from the social circle surrounding Ashley, however.

An unlikely friendship with Weedeater formed around the same time. Bonds developed beyond being my drug dealer. We started a weight lifting routine at his town house. I enjoyed riding to his home on the back of his motorcycle.

Weedeater worked as a bouncer on the weekends. His main source of income was laying cement and other masonry jobs at various construction sites. He was in his mid-twenties and had a tough exterior.

He was a kid at heart still. Besides a Harley-Davidson motorcycle, his most prized possession was a massive collection of comic books.

His favorite way to pass the time was getting stoned and reading comics. He triggered my interest in comics. We would ride to the comic book store on his Harley, act like kids in a candy store, and ride back to his town house. Then we would spend hours smoking weed and reading our new comic books.

Occasionally, we had in-depth conversations or debates about things like: the greatest characters, the best superpowers, or the perfect team. We categorize the heroes with labels such as: superhero, anti-hero, or vigilante. These conversations may have given me some inadvertent motivation.

I concocted a formula for the perfect team. The formula included: a leader, speed, agility, a powerhouse, and a wildcard. The leader might take an active role or mentor from the sidelines. Good moral fiber is mandatory for leadership. Speed speaks for itself. They show the rate of progress. In a comic book, it is called the story arc. An agile person can get in and out of any situation. They have a high tolerance for chaos also. A powerhouse has many strengths and very few negatives. They will have strong opinions and cannot be swayed. The wildcard provides a balance of power. A wildcard doesn't follow any standard operating procedure.

I embarked on a top secret mission to form the perfect team to help me complete high school. The difficult part would be choosing people with the right personalities. The field was narrowed by eliminating all the upper classes. First, I focused on other high-risk students: either who they were, or who their families were that caused them to struggle at school. Many students looked disturbed by my request.

The unexpected snag in my plan forced me to reevaluate the situation. Not every conflict will be resolved within a short period of time. I pivoted the search to find a member for a different role. Anyone in advanced classes was in contention for the powerhouse role. A few provocative possibilities piqued my interest. Toni was the obvious choice, however. She possessed a rare ability for learning. Also she haunted my dreams. I didn't want another scene at school, though.

So I went to the library to confront her. The public library felt like neutral territory. I didn't hear Toni's voice or see a group of children. Abandoning the futile search, I approached a young woman behind the large front desk counter.

"Can I help you?" She asked.

"I'd like to know if there are any classes for younger readers? I have a younger brother and he is having some trouble learning," I lied.

"Once a month a young lady reads to a group," she replied in a polite manner.

"When will she be here?"

"The schedule is on the calendar taped to the front of the counter."

The young woman leaned over and pointed down at various papers taped to the counter. I discovered the appropriate date to be every third Sunday in the month.

On that third Sunday, I observed the same woman working at the counter. I didn't really involve my brother. So I remained outside for some time.

In the meanwhile, I buried myself in meditation. I reflected on a time when my feelings for Toni were more fervent. I spent every opportunity trying to impress her in elementary school. She was the image of joviality in her early years.

One day, I attempted to impress her during recess. I started running through the playground swing set. I dodged the children swinging back and forth. My confidence built after a few successful runs. I had intended to weave through the swings without stopping. A swift-moving child hit me with his outstretched feet. I was knocked to the ground.

Toni and I waited for two empty swings next to each other. Then we had a competition to swing the highest. I leaped out of the swing at the apex. My rear end slipped out of the smooth rubber seat, my limbs thrashed, and my face made contact with the ground. I felt a gentle touch on my back. I rolled over and saw a blurred image of Toni. She leaned down to kiss the throbbing bump growing on my forehead.

We were bused into the city of Wilmington for fourth, fifth, and sixth grade. Toni showed an abnormal aptitude for subjects. She was placed in more advanced classes. Our interaction was less and less afterward.

She passed a letter to me in the hallway. Her ghostly pallor caused concern. She had cut her long lustrous hair. The new hairstyle only served to exasperate certain boyish traits at that age. I carried the letter home.

The door to my room was locked. In anguish, I studied the letter further. It rambled without giving any explanation for her anti-social behavior. My eyes wept. I crumpled the letter. I cried until no more tears came to my eyes. Then I smoothed out the letter flat. I crumpled it a second time around my nose. I took a deep breath and imagined Toni's palm resting on the paper, writing in beautiful cursive handwriting.

Finally, Toni made her exit from the library. The look on her face was defiant. My thoughts flew out of focus. I froze like a statue. She was about to disappear. Then I ran to catch her.

"You don't have to treat me like a stranger!" I called out in my pursuit.

Toni stopped walking. She turned, revealing an intimidating stare. I maintained some semblance of composure.

"Please talk to me," I continued.

"What do you want?" She asked in a frigid tone.

"I need someone to tutor me."

"Find someone else to annoy with your problems."

"You're the smartest person in the entire school. And my oldest childhood friend."

"Were you my friend?"

"Of course, I was! What are you saying?"

"You don't even remember. It was after my hair was cut short. A group of boys started calling me Elvis. Little baby Elvis. You laughed right along with them."

"I didn't laugh…"

"Well, you sure didn't stick up for me. I deserve a better friend."

"That was after…"

"After what?!"

"After you cut me out of your life."

"Ha!"

Toni closed the distance between us. The awkwardness of the situation was hard to articulate. She was like an unskilled warrior wielding a legendary weapon. Her hot breath on my face was undesired. I tripped over my own feet in an effort to maintain a comfortable distance.

She turned on her heels and walked away. I decided against any further pursuit. A ball of tension hit me with incredible force. My head dropped toward my chest. What if my plan was destined to fail?

On Monday, I returned to school without knowing whether or not anything had been accomplished. In the long crowded halls, I searched for Toni. Instead, after a few days had passed, I found a letter shoved inside my locker. The handwritten note had instructions to meet her at the public library. A specific date and time was included.

She waited outside the library, much to my surprise. Her hostile expression dared me to come close. Without warning, she punched me in the midsection. I doubled over in pain. Then she pushed me into some bushes along the walkway. As I stared with confusion, she whipped a tangle of hair away from her face.

"Now we can start over," she announced.

Toni was stoic during our study session. She disregarded any questions about her personal life. Her technique in relation to teaching was admirable, though.

She never made me feel ashamed for my ignorance. She didn't complete the work for me either.

I was forced to promise her one thing: our meetings would remain a secret. Otherwise, there would be no further meetings. She didn't want any rumors to spread, I guessed. We agreed to limit our interaction to the public library.

We continued to meet and study in the dark corners of the library. She helped expand my knowledge about a myriad of subjects. Only with her aid, was I able to complete my freshman year. Our study sessions continued after the school year ended. Toni even agreed to go roller skating during summer break.

CHAPTER 7

The 1988–1989 school year was ending. It was a warm beautiful afternoon. Most of the senior class didn't bother to attend. The few in attendance brought toilet paper and water guns. The final day was fraught with pranks and mischief.

Teacher's cars were covered with tissue. Students were pelted with rolls of toilet paper. Seniors used water guns to soak underclassmen. Many students had no special relish for such amusement. They chose to leave before the final bell.

There was a considerable number of graduation parties to attend. A total stranger extended an invitation to me. He drove to an unfamiliar neighborhood. Vacant cars lined the streets. People flocked to one house in particular. The party was already going on full tilt. I heard loud music and animated voices coming from the backyard.

We entered through a gate on the side of the house. Nobody was permitted to go inside. The graduate's mother sat inside to keep out the partygoers. I witnessed her bringing out food and drinks. There was a sophisticated spread of refreshments, including: cheese, deli meats, and a hollowed-out loaf of rye filled with spinach dip. An assortment of vegetables surrounded the loaf of rye bread. There were large coolers full of soda and beer submerged in ice. A large sheet cake sat uneaten. It looked like the cake had been smashed into the graduates' face.

I wasn't the only freshman at the party. Bradley Woodall had an older sister in the graduating class. He had brought his group of degenerates too. Brad wanted to know who invited me to the party.

"It's my cousin's party," I lied.

The backyard was filled to capacity. I stood against the back wall of the house. It was the only available space. I lost track of the person that drove me to the party. He left me to find my own way home.

The popularity contest was over for the graduates. People were being shoved into the pool fully clothed. Those with crushes acted on impulses they had resisted. A card game developed into a game of strip poker. There were teenagers in their underwear, jumping in and out of the pool.

I witnessed Ed DeFalco slip on the smooth wet concrete. He fell hard. His head made a sickening sound against the surface of the walkway. The rest of his body took an awkward trajectory toward the pool. His descent was slow. Ed's return to the surface wasn't immediate.

My response was unlike the other people. I felt mortified by the roar of laughter from the crowd. So I pushed through the crowd and jumped into the pool.

My arms latched onto Ed. His limp body came to the surface with unexpected ease due to the minimal gravity underwater. He gasped for air and escaped from my grip. I observed him swim away. Outside the pool, I attempted to render further aid. He refused my help with a violent shove.

"What are you doing?" He shouted.

"Are you okay?" I asked.

Ed didn't respond. He staggered away from the edge of the pool. I decided not to press the matter. Brad didn't miss the opportunity to make fun of his friend.

"He was hiding under the water from embarrassment," he joked.

Someone handed Ed a cold aluminum can which he held against his head. Another person directed him to sit down in a lawn chair. He was lethargic after the fall.

Ed vomited among many spectators. A gasp rose from the people around him. It was a disturbance to the partygoers trying to enjoy themselves. He ignored the complaints of disgruntled partiers. His so-called friends decided to carry him to another yard. They hoisted Ed up in the air and forced him over a nearby fence. I could hear him retching on the opposite side of the tall wooden fence. Nobody mentioned getting him medical attention. Brad was going to leave him. I followed his group to the front of the house.

"You're going to leave your friend to choke on his own vomit?" I yelled.

The driver of an awaiting vehicle stuck his head out.

"He's not going to puke in my ride!" He objected.

Brad ignored me and sat in the passenger seat. Other partygoers overheard the conversation. They wanted to get Ed out of there too. A mob formed on the front lawn. They wouldn't let the vehicle move. The crowd voiced their agitation and yelled at the driver.

"I'll check on him," Brad relented.

Brad and I stood over Ed. He lay motionless on the ground. Brad and I carried him to the car and placed him in the backseat. We were assured he wouldn't vomit. I sat next to him in the backseat. The biting odor of stomach bile forced me to roll a window down.

The drive to Four Seasons was made in silence. I offered Ed assistance to his final destination. He refused my help again. It was bewildering to watch him walk away.

At that point, I decided to invite Brad and Ed to join my study group.

CHAPTER 8

During the summer break, Toni and I met at the Christiana Skate Rink. We had to reestablish an etiquette after our long estrangement. Our unresolved issues were evident still. It was far from a perfect day.

We skated in circles for hours. Toni was quiet and subdued. I concentrated on the music, determined to appear confident. My hand brushed Toni's arm as we skated side by side. Then I clasped her hand. It was hot and sweaty like mine.

Afterward, Toni told me to wait outside. I returned my skates and stood outside in the parking lot. Toni burst through the front doors, clutching her rental skates. There was an expression of pure elation on her face.

"Come on!" She screamed.

Soon, another figure came crashing through the doors. It was the same overweight middle-aged man who had taken my skates back. There was no time for me to react as I watched the duo run past. I searched the landscape for a safe haven. There were other businesses on either side. They wouldn't provide an escape, however. There was no way for Toni to avoid getting caught.

People stopped to observe the chase in the parking lot. Her pursuer was close, inside the maze of parked cars. I approached the duo in a casual manner. She led the employee close enough to trip him with my leg. The employee fell to the ground. He toppled forward, throwing out his hands to break the fall. The employee landed on his hands and knees. Toni seized the opportunity to escape. She darted through traffic on the highway.

The employee recovered. He had small cuts on his hands from the gravel on the ground. His pants were shredded at the knees. He took a few seconds to orient himself and locate his next target. This time, I was his quarry. I sprinted at top speed away from the employee and away from Toni. He had lost some of his quickness.

Eventually, the rental desk clerk gave up his pursuit. He trudged back inside the building.

"I'm calling the cops!" were his parting words.

I reunited with Toni on the other side of the highway. We caught a bus together. She held my hand during the ride. She used her free hand to trace a figure eight on the back of my hand.

"What are you doing?" I asked.

"It's an infinity sign," she replied.

"I mean, why steal the skates?"

"Sometimes, things in life are forever. They can't be undone. Things like: family, friends, and first times can be forever. I wanted a memento from our first date."

"We're dating?"

"We never officially broke up."

Toni needed to catch a separate bus home. She lived in a development called Robscott Maner. It wasn't far from my neighborhood. A person could walk across the state of Delaware in one day. She felt far away, however. As she left the bus, I saw a glimpse of the young girl: a glimmer of the vibrant girl who stole me and my heart away from another.

The summer months were fleeting. There was a considerable amount of work to accomplish. A series of unwanted problems presented themselves. The solutions needed to be planned and executed in a short amount of time.

First, enrollment in driver's ed was automatic for sophomore students. Buying a car on my meager paperboy earnings would be impossible. So I applied for jobs at local businesses. A local convenience store provided a better paying job.

Second, my mother disappeared for over two weeks. I wasn't given any warning. One day, I found a hundred-dollar bill on the bureau in my room. She dismissed the anxiety caused by her disappearance. Later, I learned her absence had been spent at the Sturgis rally with bikers.

Furthermore, I wanted to convince three young adults to accept help. I began with some reconnaissance to obtain information. There were several interesting pieces of information. I added the facts to the matching psych profile.

I knew from our previous encounters, Brad was a typical alpha male. He treated teachers with blatant disrespect at school. His popularity wasn't widespread. He was the leader of a small group of teens with similar temperaments. That was something to be respected.

I had noticed a half pipe in his backyard while delivering papers. So I rode a skateboard around Four Seasons. It was difficult to avoid slowing down or showing too much interest around his house. There was activity on multiple occasions. Groups of teens practiced on the half-pipe almost daily.

One day, I decided to approach the chain-link fence around Brad's yard. A group watched a skater practice tricks on the half pipe. I recognized some people from school. Ed stood near the periphery of the crowd.

His was the second name on a short list of potential members. His older brother had been a star quarterback at Glasgow. He was supposed to step into his brother's cleats. He was one of those people who wanted to please everyone.

I continued to scan the crowd for Brad.

"We aren't donating to charity today."

His voice rose above the din from the crowd.

I trespassed inside his yard. The unruly crowd made it difficult to advance.

I approached Brad, clutching the skateboard in my arms. He scrutinized the board with a scowl on his face. Then he grabbed the cheap board.

"What is this?" He asked.

"That's my board," I replied.

"No. It's garbage," he said.

He placed my board right side up on the ground. Next, he stomped on the deck of the board with intense hostility. The board broke into two pieces before I had the mind to react. Instead, I chose to exit the yard and avoid a fight.

"Don't leave your garbage in my yard!" He jeered.

I retrieved the broken skateboard from the ground. Then I retreated through the crowd, receiving numerous shoves. Others jeered and stomped until I was no longer among them.

I walked toward the opposite side of the street. I stood on the sidewalk, waiting for everyone to leave. Ed exited the backyard eventually.

"What are you doing here, man?" He asked in a sympathetic tone.

"I just wanted to talk."

"With me?"

"You and Brad."

"Don't take this personal, but I don't think he likes you."

"Maybe you can convince him to accept help. I'm forming a study group…"

Ed rolled his eyes. He was overwhelmed by the urge to laugh at my suggestion.

"I thought you'd be more interested. You were an exceptional athlete on the football team. You didn't finish the season, though. It was your grades, wasn't it? You couldn't keep your GPA high enough to participate," I said.

"Spare me the lecture," he stated.

"Everybody needs help sometimes." I answered back.

The encounter was justification for my second thoughts. There was the display of undisguised animosity from Brad. Ed laughed and expressed very little enthusiasm. Similarly, Toni established her reluctance to meet with a large group. I wasn't buried by these impediments, however.

Next, I needed to persuade Toni to befriend Ashley. The plan required a touch of deception. Toni would pretend to shop for a car at a dealership owned by Ashley's family. I gave Toni the impression it was a second date.

Toni and I rode a bus into Wilmington. The route brought us within walking distance to an art gallery. We studied the art together, arm in arm inside the quaint gallery. She halted our progress to appreciate a piece at times, leaning on my arm as she carried out her observations. We occupied ourselves in this manner for a short duration. Then we strolled around the city.

I discovered a coffee shop near the car dealership. We sat at a table outside without placing an order. A conversation ensued, but my attention drifted toward the dealership. I wondered if Ashley was there.

She had told me about her plans during summer break many times. The air-conditioned dealership was her favorite place to avoid uncomfortable humid weather. Also, she learned the family business. Her knowledge of luxury vehicles was an unanticipated trait.

"What do you keep staring at?" Toni asked.

She turned in her seat, following my line of sight. I wondered how well she would deal with my request.

"Are you daydreaming about exotic cars?" She speculated.

I prepared to break my silence, knowing the moment would be ruined.

"That dealership belongs to Ashley's family. I need you to convince her to join the study group," I said.

Toni flashed a fierce look in my direction. Her intensity caused a shudder to course down my spine. Each of her pupils was like an unfathomable abyss.

"Tell me…why her?" She inquired.

"I think she is misunderstood," I explained.

"So she isn't self-centered. A spoiled brat, prancing through a field of flowers without a care in the world."

"Wouldn't you like to mentor her? You could mold her into a better version of herself."

Finally, Toni rose from her seat. She wandered into the dealership. I was enticed inside the shop by the aroma of coffee. Toni returned to her seat while I stood in line.

"I didn't get you anything," I told her.

"Let me taste your drink," she requested.

"It's vanilla chai on ice," I said.

I relinquished the drink. She returned an empty cup.

"That's really good. Can you order two more?" She said.

I came back to the table with two fresh drinks.

"How did it go?" I asked.

She produced a business card with a handwritten phone number on the back.

"Ashley was there. She didn't recognize me at first," she said.

"You aren't exactly a social butterfly," I replied.

"People lose a piece of themselves after a certain age. They fill the void with lies."

"Should I apologize? It's hard to get a read on you. Our reunion has been a gift. I don't want to jeopardize this relationship."

"Punching you seems to help."

CHAPTER 9

In the fall, I returned to Glascow High School. Glascow was not a trade school, but sophomores were required to select a "career elective." Sophomore students were scheduled for a mandatory meeting with a counselor within the first week. The counselor compiled a list of names for each attendance sheet. Afterward, the classes could convene. That allotted time was a study hall for the first week.

Meanwhile, Toni established a relationship with Ashley. She made an effort to connect, and Ashley was openhearted enough to allow Toni inside her orbit. I had no illusions about how they might become best friends. Their personalities were on opposite sides of the spectrum.

Toni's vexation was apparent in her behavior. She gave me very little acknowledgment inside the school building. Her elusive behavior only heightened the intrigue with which I was already possessed. I received a note in my locker with instructions to meet her outside during lunch. We continued to meet outside whenever the weather was pleasant.

There were many places to disappear. We went unnoticed inside the baseball/softball field dugouts. Bleachers on the football field provided concealment. Also, there were wooded areas near the school. Each note designated a different rendezvous.

On this occasion, we ventured off school grounds to a nearby historical site. Only one battle was fought in Delaware during the Civil War. An old bridge designated the battle with a plaque. The bridge spanned a creek in the wooded area behind the school. We followed the creek until the bridge came into view. Then we sat on the creek bed and ate our lunch.

"I'll be glad to end this charade," Toni stated.

"Are you having second thoughts?" I inquired.

"Always."

"Have you thought about sleeping with me?"

"And leave Ashley to fend for herself? I'm not that cruel."

"I thought you might smother her with a pillow."

"The majority of the group has the same curriculum. I have a tentative lesson plan and exercises to perform, if anyone accepts the invitation. I need a long narrow board for the first exercise. Are your parents aware of your plan?"

"My parents are divorced. My mom will go along with the plan if parents called the house. I explained everything. She was eager to meet my friends."

"Friends!? You know these people publicly? There are certain rules of social grace to be followed in public. In private…people are different."

Graphic arts was the only elective suitable to me. Coincidentally, Ed chose the same elective. He sat in the desk next to mine. Being in the same elective with him turned out to be more fun than I expected.

At first, I was bored by the work. The task of drawing a structure in order to learn perspective seemed mundane. I learned to enjoy the simple exercise, however. The neatness of the ordered lines excited my imagination. I admired the stark beauty of planes and angles.

Ed didn't have the aptitude of a draftsman. He required my help with some of the projects. I seized every opportunity to change his opinion about the study group. My persistence swayed his position. He agreed to extend an invitation to Brad also.

Finally, everyone had been invited to stay overnight. It was impossible to predict how many people would accept the invitation. My uneasiness was attributed to this fact. The incessant uncertainty drove a torrent of adrenaline into my bloodstream. I paced the floor in my bedroom. At intervals, I stopped to peer through the blinds.

Toni arrived at my house first. My mother met her outside without any instruction. She escorted Toni to my room. I was eager to remove her from the rigorous scrutiny of my mother.

"If you want to talk some more, I can get a bright light to shine in her face," I said.

Half an hour later, Brad and Ed were at my house. They didn't bother to bring any books. The way they scanned my bedroom made me want to hide anything of value. I was too preoccupied to notice Ashley's arrival.

My mother went to the shiny new BMW parked at the curb. Toni hurried outside to greet Ashley too. I observed from my bedroom window as my mother encouraged the girls to go inside the house. Then she started a conversation with Ashley's father.

I turned away from the window, detecting Ashley's presence in my room. A moment of tense silence followed as everyone awaited her first statement. Her eyes shifted toward each individual in an effort to determine their identity. Toni brushed by her and entered the room.

"What are they doing here?" Ashley asked.

"It's my house," I responded.

"There is something very wrong with this scenario. Is this kidnapping? Why did you lure me here?" She continued.

"I'm starting a study group," I explained.

Ashley stormed out of the room straightaway. I took another glance through the blinds and noticed the BMW was gone. Then I went to find her; we collided in the hall. She realized her father had left, changed directions, and pushed me aside.

"Please, just hear me out," I begged.

"I told you to never speak to me again. I need to use your phone," she stated.

"Don't you want to go back to the private school? Which colleges will accept you now?" I inquired.

I followed her back inside my room. She didn't use the phone to call for a ride home. Instead, she confronted Toni.

"Why did you agree to this? Don't you have a 4.0 GPA?" She questioned.

"I didn't have anything better to do," Toni said.

"Exactly. I'm the only relevant person in this room. I don't need to be part of this group of misfit rejects!" Ashley insisted.

Brad occupied himself, rummaging through my music collection. Ashley's outburst didn't deter his search. Although, he wasn't about to allow her slanderous remark go unanswered.

"Enjoy it while it lasts," he stated.

"Did you say something, miscreant?" She replied.

"There are two types of fat people: ones that are born fat and others that have a fat person lurking inside. I can see that fatty lurking inside you."

He inflated his cheeks and made a gesture to simulate expanding.

"Little boys are so stupid. You use asinine games of intimidation to push people around. Believe it or not, you can't bully your way to success," Toni scolded him.

"You want some too? Freak show." Brad asked.

"Hey! How about a time-out?" I shouted.

"Oh, did I hit a nerve? I can see why you like her so much. She's got that whole painted whore thing going," Brad snapped.

"Brad and Ed can help me get some snacks from the kitchen," I suggested.

"Yeah. I'm sure the porker is hungry," Brad quipped.

They followed me out of the room. Brad made pig noises as he left. In the kitchen, I removed cans of soda and juice boxes from the refrigerator. Then I placed them on the counter. My entire body vibrated with tension. I spun around to face Brad, grabbing his jacket with both hands. A low growl rumbled from deep within. "Don't!" I warned him. He forced me to lose my grip on his jacket.

"Girls like it when you throw shade on them. They like it—it's banter," he explained.

"I want you to apologize," I revealed.

There was an old cigarette pack inside a pocket of my jeans. It contained: a few joints and a lighter. I extracted the cigarette pack from my pocket, handed it to Brad, and he opened it.

"Apologize to the girls and convince them to smoke," I said.

"Why? Cause they expect it from me. You fraud."

"These next two years are going to make or break you. A real man can admit he doesn't know everything and accept help."

"I'm going to tolerate that remark because I want to get zoned out. You ever put your hands on me again, you'll be drinking your meals through a straw."

Brad and Ed exited the kitchen. They neglected to carry any food or drinks. Upon entering my room, Brad relieved me of one provision. He made himself comfortable on my bed, turned on the TV with the remote, and tore open the bag of chips. Our return drew very little attention from the girls.

Toni and Ashley stood in front of my closet. Articles of clothing were strewn on the floor. Ashley held a dress shirt. She gave Toni a look and they both laughed. The shirt was discarded on the floor. Next, Toni removed my favorite dark gray Abercrombie pullover hoodie from the closet.

"Benji, can I have this?" She asked.

"Don't ever call me that again," I said. Toni and Ashley removed more items.

"Can I have this?" They repeated.

"Pick one thing," I told them.

Brad gained everyone's attention after we heard the friction wheel grind against a flint inside the lighter. He repeated the action over and over. Finally, I observed him ignite the butane and set fire to a joint. He inhaled a rapid series of puffs from the joint. The movement of air created a large flame. He blew it out like a birthday candle. The flame was extinguished, and the joint burned more even.

"You can't come into someone's house and do drugs," Toni reprimanded.

"It's not a problem, Toni. My mom's biker friends have been doing drugs," I said.

"You crave attention so much. You don't care it's the negative type," Toni continued.

"You're bringing me down, Freak show. Hit this joint and relax," Brad said.

"Try again," I interrupted.

"I'm sorry for my earlier behavior. There's no filter between my brain and my mouth," he added.

"It would be another first for you," I offered.

Toni accepted the joint, inhaled a tiny puff of smoke, and exhaled. She never removed her contemptuous stare from Brad.

"Sincere or not, I leave forgiveness to God," she stated.

Ashley reminded me of a cigarette ad, holding the joint. She brought the joint to her lips in an extravagant manner. The pretentious scene was ruined after she began to cough.

"Oh my God!" She croaked. "Give me a juice box."

"That is the sound virgin lungs make," I laughed.

"Why don't you tell us, Ben?" Brad questioned.

"Does Ashley have any virgin parts left?"

"Where the rumors true or not?" Ed pressed.

"Did something happen between you two last year? Or is the head of the Glascow glam squad a modest prude?" Brad continued.

"Just tell us, Ashley," Ed added.

"No!" Ashley screamed. "I've never done it!"

"It was me." Toni revealed.

Her hand was raised like she wished to be called on in class.

"I made up the rumor and wrote on your locker," she continued.

My eyes grew wide. I had no reply to this revelation. Everyone remained quiet for a while. The silence was profound. Ashley broke the palpable silence, eventually.

"This will never work," she stated.

"On Monday, Brad is going to cut all of us down. Ed will be his flunky, still. Ben can fade into the background. Toni can stop spreading lies and this twisted game can end."

"The princess is right, Benji. This glimpse into your pathetic life isn't amusing enough for a repeated exploration," Brad added.

Ashley appeared to be on the verge of tears. She might have been overwhelmed by the circumstances, or this was another persuasive act. Toni dumped the contents of her overnight bag onto the floor. She grabbed a large sanitary pad and offered it to Ashley.

"It's super absorbent," Toni disclosed.

"That's bizarre," Brad stated.

"Sorry, I don't have any tears for you outcasts," Ashley announced.

"I'm not good at emotional support. I don't have any friends," Toni replied.

"Are we friends?" Ashley inquired.

"Right here and right now," I responded.

"Anarchy will be the new normal," Brad declared.

He lit another joint. Then he flipped off the lights. I was grateful to receive the second joint. The first one never made the journey. A large portion of the weed was consumed by flames. Intoxication washed away every splinter of pain around my temple region. I closed my eyes and felt my breath rise and fall.

"Where did you go, Ben?" Toni's voice echoed.

"My happy place," I answered.

"I don't feel any different," she said.

I studied her through squinted eyes. A flicker of light danced around the outer limits of her body. The curves of her body were hidden by my favorite pullover.

"You are different," I told her.

"What do you mean?" She asked.

"You are right. People are different in private. I noticed the difference in you, mostly. This was a bad idea from the start to finish. Will you help me through graduation, still?"

"I'm here for you."

Eventually, Toni and I used my textbooks to study. The general reading wasn't the most important matter in my opinion. Toni's strict attentiveness and support was the most helpful. It was a triumph to have her as a friend.

Afterward, she gave instruction on test taking methods. Her examples would help anticipate key issues. An intersecting revelation occurred to me. The others were attentive during her brief lecture.

The only interruption was a loud growl from Ed's stomach. The girls offered to cook breakfast for everyone. "We want it to be edible," Toni explained. They ransacked the kitchen for provisions.

Toni had a specific meal in mind. She found the necessary ingredients and made banana pancakes. The meal included every piece of sausage and bacon in the house. Instead of maple syrup, I used chocolate syrup. Toni sprinkled powder sugar on her pancakes. Everyone was lethargic after they had gorged themselves on the delicious food.

"Are you going to feed us like this every time?" Ed inquired.

"I'm not going to let anyone starve," I replied.

"I'm talking about the pancakes Toni made. I could eat them every day: breakfast, lunch, and dinner," Ed stated.

"It can be a tradition," Toni said.

"We should vote," Ashley announced.

"Raise your hand if you want to continue meeting."

"Everyone is just going to drink the Kool-Aid!? You think Ben can make us better citizens?" Brad questioned.

"Are you done?" Ashley asked.

"Let's make it official."

Her hand was in the air already. She made a disgruntled facial expression. I wanted to kick everyone—not including Toni—out on the street. Regardless, I raised my hand. Toni and Ed signed their approval. Of course, Brad made everyone else wait for his response. His vote meant the resolution was unanimous.

CHAPTER 10

The second study session began with an activity. The objective was to traverse a 2×4. The piece of lumber was ten feet long. We each endeavored to accomplish the task ten times and recorded the results after each attempt.

"This is ridiculous." Brad declared.

"This is a proven method." Toni insisted.

"Imagine you're a gymnast on a balance beam, or walking on the ledge of a building thirty stories in the air. It's a concentration exercise, and it wakes up the brain."

"How about we try it stoned?" I suggested.

"You have weed?" Toni asked.

"It helps me concentrate," I explained.

Everyone repeated the exercise under the influence of marijuana. The results were interesting. The second trial was completed with a more concerted effort. I enjoyed the competition.

Afterward, each individual studied for an hour or more. Toni was a source of aid to anyone with a question. Her demeanor was different with each individual. She was firm with Brad, patient with Ed, and more reliant on participation from Ashley. She was nurturing at the same time, imparting self-reliance. Observing her special qualities made everything worthwhile.

My hasty looks didn't go unnoticed. She raised an eyebrow, but displayed very little interest in flirtation. Her nose crinkled as she concentrated on her own studies.

"It's odd, isn't it? Ben made the night sky light up like fireworks for me. Has he done anything special for you, Toni?" Ashley gloated.

"We have our shared experiences," Toni said.

"You should buy something nice for her, Ben. We can go to the mall tomorrow," Ashley advised.

Saturday morning, the entire group rode the bus to Christiana Mall. There were no other passengers on the bus. We sat far apart. Toni's mood was sullen. No one had much to say. The silence felt uncomfortable.

Inside the mall, we followed Ashley. She wandered in and out of her favorite shops. Brad and Ed grew bored of the flowering boutiques and gaudy outlets. They voiced their discontent after everyone stopped near one of the huge fountains.

"We can meet you in the food court later," Brad said.

"We didn't come along to hold your purses while you shop," Ed added.

I kept my opinion to myself. It was still unspoken, but something was on Toni's mind. Her icy blue eyes were cast upon me with intense scrutiny. She came closer and spoke to me in a brusque manner.

"Give me your money," she demanded.

"You're just going to pick something out?" I inquired.

"No. I want you to steal something," she replied.

I gave her all the money on my person. The money was meant to go toward a car. I quit my paper route to start the study group. A clerk position at a convenience store was more lucrative. Toni and Ashley departed after I relinquished my money.

Brad and Ed were brazen enough to reach into the fountain and remove coins from the bottom. They filled their pockets with pilfered coins. Ed had a grin on his face.

"Don't steal anything around us. You'll probably get caught," he warned.

"That's ironic," I responded.

They took the coins to an arcade inside the mall. I watched as they played video games. After a while, I left their company.

It was a difficult task, ascertaining an item. I wandered from store to store. Most store employees were wary of an unaccompanied minor. I felt like other shoppers were suspicious of my movements also. The paranoia was too much to bear.

My mind was a beehive of activity. I was overwhelmed by the uneasy state of mind. So I hurried to the food court. One thought annoyed me more than any other. How much would my failure amuse Brad and Ed?

They waited at a table in the food court. Trays full of food from multiple restaurants crowded the table. They gorged themselves on a banquet of fast food. "Show us what you stole." Brad asked the question between bites. I shrugged and presented my empty hands.

They began to mock me with a boisterous laugh. I made one or two clever retorts as they commenced my belittlement. The language they used to discredit my witticism was cruel. They ceased their torment after the girls came into view.

Toni and Ashley approach the table, carrying numerous bags from various stores. Their movements were further hindered by multiple layers of apparel. I presumed the additional clothing was stolen. My suspicion was confirmed as they identified which items were stolen.

"What about the rules of social grace?" I asked Toni.

"Shoplifting is a cultural skill," she stated. "I refuse to be repressed by society's code of conduct. Society is the root of all evil, not money."

"Tony and I are going to meet my father out front. We are not riding public transit with all these bags," Ashley explained.

CHAPTER 11

A little past eight o'clock, doubt crept into my mind. Brad and Ed had not arrived for the study session. I wanted to start without them, but the girls advised patience was the proper course. I sought to distract my agitated mind. My irritability subsided as I rolled a blunt.

Ashley scrutinized my progress while she conversed with Toni. Her eyes focused on the movement of my hands. I planned to test her skill. A vigorous knock on the front door diverted my intent.

It was a few minutes past nine in the evening. Another insistent knock was delivered to the door. Brad and Ed disturbed the stillness of the evening. I looked at the pair for a moment, showing some reluctance to allow them to enter.

Now, matters could proceed with everyone present. Toni used flash cards to drill individuals. It was a simple exercise. Ed recorded the results.

Next, he created a file for each person. Grades from our school assignments were added to the files. Toni helped to calculate averages for each person.

In the meantime, I taught Ashley to roll a blunt. I took her hands in mine and issued instructions to pinch the ends of the cigar wrapper. "Work your way toward the middle as you twist it closed," I instructed. She didn't allow any weed to escape, and the wrapper was kept tight. I was impressed with the results of her effort.

"Girls must be better suited for this. Our fingers are more nimble," she said.

A flicker of annoyance passed over Toni's face. She gained possession of an oversized black marker from her bag. Then she wrote

Einstein's theory of relativity on my bedroom wall. I watched her vandalize the wall in shock.

"This is a fact we are all familiar with." She said.

"It's a theory." Brad interrupted.

"My point is this: most people aren't blank slates. A person can be influenced, but they can't be changed. The challenge is to comprehend how a person perceives and responds to the world. Then arrive at the best way to manipulate the innate disposition to bring about desired behaviors," she explained.

At first, I was too concerned about the wall to understand any lesson with accuracy. I did appreciate the authority she was endowed with, however. It would take me years to learn that kind of assuredness. She was able to transform the most transparent person, so they couldn't recognize themselves.

"It's exactly what you're attempting, Benji," she continued.

"What did I do now?" I asked.

Toni gave me a look. "Create a Pavlovian response," she expounded.

"What's that?" Ed asked.

"Pavlov was a psychologist. He fed dogs treats after a bell was rung. Soon, the dogs salivated without the introduction of food. He used positive reinforcement to create a new behavior," she stated.

"I was stoned out of my mind when I had the idea for this study group. I was inspired by my desperation. I felt empty inside after my parents divorced. Drugs filled the void, but I couldn't stand to be alone with myself," I announced.

The rest of the evening was uneventful. After two hours of individual study time, Toni and Ashley went into my brother's old room.

The following evening, Ashley arrived at my house alone. She caused a disturbance outside my bedroom window. The loud noise startled me. So I peered through the blinds to discover the source. Ashley stood on the front lawn, brushing debris off herself. I opened the front door and allowed her inside. She went into my room and sat on the bed without saying a word.

"Are you okay? What happened?" I inquired.

"I couldn't reach your window because of the bushes. I fell into the side of the house," She explained.

"Why are you here?"

"I wanted to smoke weed."

I was apprehensive about her sudden appearance. She kept adjusting herself. She turned her head as if she were looking at something in the room. I noticed a twig clinging to her hair and liberated it. Her hair color was somewhere between rust and gold. It was hard to determine in certain light.

"Do you want me to roll something up?" She asked.

"Yeah," I responded.

We passed a blunt back and forth. I searched her face for clues to any ulterior motives. Her cheeks had a pink hue like two pink roses. She flipped her hair away from the right side of her face. A pleasant aroma of berries wafted in my direction. There was a bouquet of intermingling fragrances.

Her perfume smelled like honeysuckle. We were close enough for me to smell the baby powder-scented deodorant she wore. We were two normal teens with sexual tension. All the feelings I had for her were right there on the surface. As long as I never acted on those feelings, everything would be fine.

"Do you ever wonder—what if?" She asked.

There was a pause before the next question.

"Have you ever been with anyone?"

"As in having sex? No."

"It's a great high."

"But I thought…"

"Please, you fell for that act? I tell everybody they're the first."

"Please, don't say anything."

Her expression was a relief. It showed neither surprise or disappointment.

"I'll tell you a secret, and we'll be even," she began. At Caravel, I kissed one of my field hockey teammates. We were celebrating a win. Rumors circulated the school. That's one of the reasons my grades were so poor."

"Is that true?" I asked.

"Maybe. Do you want to see my pj's?"

Ashley didn't wait for my response. She left the room with a designer bag. I stood by my bed and waited for her return. She strutted out of the bathroom, wearing a pink and white nightie. It failed to conceal her pink silk panties.

"What do you think?" She asked.

"I think Toni will get details of everything that takes place tonight."

"What's one more secret between us?"

"I also think everyone in the group should avoid sex with each other."

"That will never pass a vote."

We made ourselves comfortable on my bed. The level of comfort in our association didn't give me a sense of ease. Ashley opened up about her personal life more and more. She explained how her father purchased expensive gifts to gain favor. I thought we might talk and smoke weed until the sun shone outside. Fatigue struck us both, however.

"I'm ready for my pj's, too," I said.

Ashley helped me remove my clothes, handling each article with tenderness. Then she flung the clothes as if the items displeased her. I watched her eyes roam about my body, glancing down to my boxers. Her right hand caressed my smooth chest.

Suddenly, she grabbed my manhood with her free hand. I stumbled backward to escape her grip. There was a triumphant smile on her face. She positioned herself with one hand on her hip. The opposite hand brushed the delicate skin on her thigh.

I hurried to throw on some pajama bottoms. They failed to conceal the bulge that lingered underneath.

She leaned closer to me with her eyes shut.

"What are you doing?" I asked.

"Not even a good night kiss? You're breaking my heart. Do you love Toni?"

"She's my first love."

I looked into Ashley's eyes, searching for any signs of hurt. Instead, I saw a glint of mischievousness paired with a wry smile on her lips. She gave my genitals a violent tap. The pain nauseated my stomach.

"Nice cock!" She laughed.

Then she pranced out of the room. I had a thought she might try to come back into the room during the night.

In the morning, Ashley returned from my brother's old room. She hovered above my face and startled me awake. "Let's wake and bake!" She implored. I pulled the covers over my head and turned away from her. The mention of marijuana was enough to motivate me, however.

Our course was set—we got high and ate breakfast together. Here my visitor offered one last question for consideration. "You don't have any regrets?"

"If I survive high school, ask me that same question," I replied.

On Monday, I met Toni in the cafeteria. She sat down next to me at our regular table. I watched her hands in case she made a fist.

"I know you lied," she began. "You gave the weed to Brad at the first meeting."

"Did he mention it?"

"Secrets will undo our relationship."

"My dreams won't come true without you in my life."

"That sounds so selfish. You lit up the sky for her."

I had no response to offer Toni. The conversation wasn't over, however. She walked with me through the hallways, only to ambush me in a secluded area of the school. Her forearm pinned me against the wall. I felt like a feral animal had cornered me. A look devoid of any human characteristics was in her eyes; she was indifferent to my pain or pleasure.

"Do you have a gun?" She asked.

"Are you plotting something?"

"You'd never see it coming. Just answer the question."

"I have a BB gun."

"I need it for an exercise."

"Is there something else?"

I expected an end to this uncomfortable situation. Instead, I received another violent shove into the wall.

"Brad asked me on a date," she replied.

With that, she removed her forearm and walked away. I allowed her to walk a safe distance from my location, so I wouldn't receive any further injuries to my internal organs. There was no method to placate her. Her behavior reminded me of the first time I saw her.

The study group continued to convene on a regular basis. Everyone continued to smoke weed. Each individual developed a preferred method. Different types of paraphernalia were brought to the meetings.

Toni and I preferred to give each other hits of smoke via the shotgun method. She presented the strategy as a contest at first. "How far can you stretch one hit?" She questioned. First, she placed a lit amber inside her mouth. Thick smoke poured out of the opposite end of the cigar wrapper. Second, I filled my lungs with smoke. Next, she brought her lips close to mine. The cycle was completed after I exhaled the smoke into her mouth.

For a moment, she held her breath. I waited with anticipation for her exhalation. She blew a tiny part of smoke into my eyes. The natural instinct was to wince and close my eyes. I felt her hands caress my face. Then she pressed her lips against mine.

She delivered a few soft kisses to my lips. Then her tongue jutted inside my mouth. A flavor like toasted marshmallows danced on my taste buds. She sucked on my lower lip after our tongues were finished gently circling. I savored her unbelievable kiss.

The following week, Toni conducted a new exercise. She wanted to avoid the Dick and Jane syndrome of education. The exercise took place in my backyard. Cans with letters taped on the side were erected in a row. Toni read a question followed by three possible answers to a member of the group. In response the group member shot a can labeled: A, B, or C.

CHAPTER 12

That year, my father married his second wife. The bride wasn't the young college student, Stacy. I knew very little about his new wife. I wasn't invited to the wedding ceremony.

I experienced feelings of alienation. There was something so pretentious about the new family unit. The woman had a daughter my age. So they moved into a house larger than the previous one.

I didn't spend much time as a guest after they moved into the new house. It hurt to be separated from my brother for long durations of time. I felt sad as I passed his empty room. The room had remained empty until the girls started to use it on the weekends.

I just wanted to be happy. Binge drug use was my prescription for a carefree time. The real enjoyment was sharing the experience with my extended family. The study group continued in the regular fashion until we had our own transportation.

Reluctantly, I bought a 1986 Mercury Topaz. All the expenses were paid with my own money: tags, insurance, and inspection fees. The car was clean and the mileage was low. It belonged to my grandmother. My mother brokered the deal. I gave her a thousand dollars and she brought the car to the house. Later, I discovered the car was meant to be a gift.

Of course, Ashley was the first to acquire a vehicle. She ordered a brand-new Mercedes from her father's dealership. She drove us to most places in her car.

Newark was a college town. Main Street was the heart of the campus. Every weekend, people crowded the area. The streets were congested; traffic came to a standstill. It was better to park in the Newark shopping center or University Plaza and walk.

Crowds liked to frequent a pizzeria on Main Street. Ripe Tomatoes had the best slice of pizza in Newark. The parking lot filled to capacity with exotic vehicles: trucks, muscle cars, and street race cars. They had high tech accessories, modifications, and expensive audio equipment. It was near impossible to obtain a parking space in front of the pizza shop. Ashley made many failed attempts to procure a space for her Mercedes.

The novelty of driving in circles faded fast. College students vacated campus during summer break. Brad grew restless after classes were dismissed. He suggested a late-night excursion.

He refused to divulge any details about the journey. Despite the secrecy, his suggestion passed a vote. So everyone left my room and piled into Ashley's car. I felt squeezed by the other boys in the rear seat.

Brad leaned forward, peering through the windshield. He gave directions to the northbound on-ramp of I-95.

Ashley drove toward the city of Wilmington. "Take this exit," Brad demanded. Ashley followed his directions to our final destination.

Soon we arrived at a secluded section of the city. Ashley parked a short distance from a construction site. A skeleton building stood out in the remote area. The structure towered above the surrounding buildings.

Everyone crawled underneath a temporary fence around the site. A deep trench encompassed the structure's foundation. The gap was bridged with a piece of lumber. Then Brad offered his hand to Toni. She grabbed his hand and he shuffled to the middle of the board. I watched in a state of bewilderment as they dashed across the gap together.

They proceeded to climb a central staircase. My ascent was slow. The wind gained strength as I climbed each flight of stairs. Steel girders were exposed to the open air. The upper levels and rooftop remained unfinished.

The others awaited me on the concrete slab overhead. I stopped at the foot of the final flight of stairs. My heartbeat was palpable.

After a brief respite, I sprinted up the stairs, leaping over some stairs in my path.

I perceived all that could be seen, but my focus was drawn to Toni. Her arm was extended like she could touch an object above. Moonlight illuminated her face. She was surrounded by the rest of the group. They stood in a cluster. Toni named visible objects in the dark firmament. Everyone except Brad was oblivious to my emergence from the lower level.

Brad noticed my presence. He lit a joint. It was passed among us. "You made it," He announced. "This is what I call getting high." Next, he edged closer to a corner of the concrete slab. His actions made me nervous. He clutched a steel girder and leaned over the tremendous height.

There was a clear panorama of the city skyline. The view was breathtaking. Nothing could have tempted me to be within ten feet of the edge, however. I braced myself for every gust of wind, afraid I might be swept off my feet.

The girls were anxious for a change of scenery. They hurried toward the stairs. Their gait was unsteady. I had an eagerness to feel the earth under my feet also.

"What's wrong?" Brad asked. He had left his dangerous perch, scrambled across the concrete slab, and blocked my path. My knees trembled too much to outmaneuver him.

"Why don't you sell the weed?" He continued.

"I'm too busy with schoolwork," I replied.

"You haven't had sex with either of the girls?"

"No."

"You're a cherry?"

"Sex with yourself doesn't count," Ed added.

"Do you think Toni has her cherry?" Brad asked.

There wasn't an opportunity to make a response. A bright flash of light from the street below drew our attention. Ashley's car turned and headed away from the construction site. Brad and Ed concluded it was time to leave.

Ed was able to reach the temporary fence first. Brad was ahead of me on the stairs by a narrow margin. I pushed him as we raced down to the ground floor. He pushed me from behind. I tumbled down a few steps to the landing below.

I was able to recover rather quick from the fall. There was no chance for him to escape. Before he concluded his descent, I reclaimed my position. Then I landed a sucker punch.

I couldn't refrain from violence. As we approached the ground floor, I surprised Brad with a hard strike on his right cheekbone. We wrestled on the final flight of stairs, lost our balance, and rolled down the remaining steps. A deep animosity fueled our struggle.

We tore at each other. I latched onto his upper arm, locating the median nerve. I pressed the nerve against the humerus bone with my thumb. He screamed in pain. Then he retaliated with a violent kick. His attack forced me to release him.

He attempted to leave. I charged him like a rampant bull. Our bodies collided we both fell. We fell through a gaping hole in the concrete slab. The hole was an access to the sublevel. We dropped around fifteen feet. I landed on top of him.

Again, he screamed in pain. We landed on a pile of scrap lumber. I removed myself from his limp body. A moan escaped his lips. As much as I wanted to leave him, I was oblivious to the full extent of his injuries, and our departure would be hampered without my aid.

I thrust my hand into his and pulled with great effort. He didn't budge from his position. "I can't move," he stated. Next, I pushed him with both hands, rolling him onto his stomach. A board was fastened to his back by nails embedded in the piece of lumber. He was able to move after the board had been removed from his posterior. We vacated the construction site and searched for the others.

Eventually, Ashley drove back to the area. She was in a jovial mood at first. Then she noticed a dark stain on Brad's shirt. A small amount of blood dribbled from his mouth.

"Is that blood?" Ashley yelled.

I was about to explain when Brad interrupted.

"It was dark and I fell," he said.

"Don't get it all over my car!" She demanded.

Ashley sped to my house. Toni tended to Brad's injuries in the bathroom. She wiped the small puncture wounds with alcohol pads. Brad had bitten his tongue. It wasn't serious enough to require stitches. The main concern was a concussion.

Two weeks later, Brad wanted to go on another late-night excursion. This outing was planned for the following weekend. He revealed the details to the rest of us. He wanted to commit another crime. Instead of trespassing on private property, Brad suggested a home invasion.

"I overheard my parents talking about a couple in the neighborhood. They'll be in the Bahamas for a weeklong vacation," Brad said.

"So?" Ashley replied.

"So we should find out where they keep their valuables," he explained.

Toni and I looked at each other. Her demure countenance didn't mask the glint of excitement in her eyes. I wanted to learn the motive behind her behavior.

"What?" She whispered.

"It's not right," I mumbled.

"Does he speak for you?" Brad asked Toni.

"I agree with him," she answered.

"I'm down," Ed announced.

"It's on you, Ashley," Brad commented.

Ashley relished her control over the group. She took a long dramatic pause. Then she cast the deciding vote.

"We're doing it!" She exclaimed.

Toni beckoned me aside.

"We don't have to go with them," she offered.

"Why do you enjoy stealing so much?" I asked.

The other voices in my room were a low murmur in the back of my mind. I studied Toni's face. There was a hint of sadness in her expression. It implied she knew the ugly side of life. I reached out to comfort her, but she gently pushed my arm away.

"Have you ever lost something or someone?" She began.

"Of course," I said.

"It's the exact opposite feeling. I might be a kleptomaniac. The criminally insane break the social contract more than other people."

"You don't always communicate on a level I can understand. I just want to connect with you on some level."

"I'm here for you, aren't I?"

"Can we show the others there is a better way to do things?"

"I'll come up with something."

"If we're not all in jail by then."

We rejoined the others to hear Brad's plan. His scrupulousness was evident as he gave a descriptive report of the objective. He instructed Ed to draw a blueprint of the two-story house. Also, items needed to complete the objective were compiled in a list.

The following Friday, we prepared to burglarize a home. Brad assured us the house was unoccupied. Everyone changed into dark apparel. We all looked very similar in our monochromatic outfits.

Everyone gathered at the front door. Brad gestured for Ed to stand next to him. "Ed and I will leave first. Wait ten minutes, maintain a sizable distance, and don't act suspect. So nobody reports a gang of teenagers roaming the streets at three a.m." He velcroed a black ski mask around the bottom half of his face. Then Brad and Ed left my house.

I observed the girls make their final adjustments. Toni wore the hoodie she took from my closet. She tucked her ponytail inside the hood and pulled the strings tight. Ashley hid her hair under a black wool hat. They both wore black spandex pants. The ten minutes elapsed, and they went to search for the rendezvous point.

I was too impatient to wait another ten minutes. I left my house and walked through the neighborhoods at a rapid pace. My pace slowed after the girls were visible. I followed the distant figures to a wooded region. The entire group assembled in a place that was unobservable from the residential area.

It was an opaque night. A touch of humidity sweetened the air. The moon was hidden by a blanket of clouds. The dark woods felt like an eerie place in the twilight hour. There were no dogs in the neighboring yards to sound an alarm. Yet, my nerves threatened to unravel.

"I'm going to gain entry. One by one, follow me inside," Brad instructed.

His words were muffled by the mask. He held a finger to his mask, warning us to stay quiet. I observed him scurry toward the house. His body was hunched over as he rushed to a side door. He pried the door apart from the doorjamb. Then he vanished from sight.

"Who's next?" Ed asked.

Suddenly, Toni bolted toward the entry point. Her petite frame looked like a woodland fairy emerging from the forest. She darted across the grass with the playfulness of a cute little kitten. After she was inside, Ashley ran in the same direction.

Ed and I played rock, paper, scissors, to be the next person inside. Ed won. I waited for him to step through the doorway. Then I ran to the house as fast as possible.

I charged into the garage. Ed lurked in the dark, searching for anything valuable. He was able to shut the door even though it had been splintered by the crowbar. The door to the residence had a broken pane of glass. I entered into the kitchen and heard an abundance of noise.

There were a variety of sounds throughout the house. I heard floorboards creak, individuals rummaged through furniture, and something fell to the floor. My ears differentiated between the sounds and soft voices.

In the living room, I was unnerved by countless tiny eyes. They stared back amidst the darkness. A large Hummel collection was kept in a tail cabinet. I inspected small tables full of figurines, shelves of marionettes, and porcelain dolls arranged with care on the couch.

"Creepy, right?" Toni whispered.

Her lips were very close to my ear. I was startled by her close proximity. She wrapped her arms around my torso. Then her hands crept downward.

"Are you excited?" She inquired.

"What's going on in here?" Ed interrupted.

I jumped and my breath hitched again. Ed had completed his search of the garage. He stepped forward, gazing at the legion of miniature figures. We were joined by Brad and Ashley.

They came down from the second floor. Ashley let her eyes drift around the room. Brad voiced his discontent. "Are you even trying?" He urged. The entire group moved into the kitchen.

Brad opened cabinet doors. His investigation uncovered a cabinet full of liquor. He selected a bottle and poured the contents down his throat. I motioned for Toni to follow me out of the kitchen. We ran upstairs.

Photos lined the hallway. I couldn't escape a feeling that I recognized the homeowners. I imagined what they might be like in their day-to-day life. I wondered how they would react, knowing their home had been invaded.

First, we entered the master bedroom. It was clear someone had rummaged through the room in an effort to find something. I didn't intend to steal anything—I only studied the interior of the room.

Next, I went room to room. A shiny object on the desk caught my eye. It was a letter opener. The room could have been used as an office or study.

"What did you find?" Toni asked.

"Do you think this is solid gold or gold plated?"

"We'll find out later."

She took the object and placed it inside her pocketbook. Then she searched the room. Some other items were deemed valuable. A Polaroid camera piqued her interest. She took a photo of me in the dark room. I threw my hands in front of my face.

"Don't do that!" I scolded.

"It works," She replied.

Ed appeared in the doorway.

"You gotta come see this!" He exclaimed.

He ushered us to the entrance of the master bedroom. He stopped short of the doorway and allowed us to pass. I took the first step across the threshold. My eyes scanned the interior. Brad and Ashley were rudely fucking on the homeowners' bed. The image seared itself inside my brain.

Torn between the mesmerizing deed and the urgent impulse to leave, I couldn't move. "Stop that," Toni reprimanded. Even though she stared straight at me, I suspected she had given the two people on the bed an instruction. Regardless, she pulled me out of the room by my arm. Then she flung me out in front and pushed me forward. She guided me downstairs into the dining room.

Eventually, the others joined us. Brad had a locked security box tucked under his arm. Ashley hugged a change holder shaped like an oversized crayon. We secured the rest of our loot and made an escape. Each person walked a different route to my house.

I followed Toni outside. She turned to acknowledge my presence with a playful wave. Quick as a startled deer, she ran toward a pitch-black area. I hurried to the edge of the darkness. I listened for any noise, but heard no sign of her.

I walked the rest of the way alone. She waited for me on the front lawn of my house. She was barefoot and danced on the grass.

"The dew tickles my toes," she laughed.

"I love you, Toni."

"I want your face to be the very last thing I see before I die."

"You couldn't just tell me…"

"Come on. Let me inside. I want to take a better picture of you."

Toni and I went to my room. We decided to inspect the stolen items. I admired a colorful silk scarf as she sorted jewelry. There were handfuls of jewelry: necklaces, earrings, bracelets, and rings. The pieces were 10K or 24K gold with precious and semi-precious stones. A tap on my bedroom window occurred as she decorated herself with jewelry.

Ed waited outside for me to open the front door. I hurried him inside the house. Brad and Ashley were visible further down the street. Ashley joined Toni in my room. The rest of us brought the security box to the basement.

We broke the security box open with a hammer and chisel. A .38 revolver spilled out of the box and clattered across the floor. Brad rushed to snatch the pistol off the floor. I was relieved the box contained no ammunition. The way Brad waved the pistol around caused me new concern. Then he opened the cylinder, revealing the absence of bullets.

"What are you going to do with that?" Ed asked.

"Oh, I'm keeping this," Brad stated.

"The rest is going to the pawn shop, right?" Ed continued.

"Yeah. We'll split the money," Brad answered.

The situation only worsened. I was called in to cover another clerk's shift. He had quit his job after being robbed at gunpoint. I imagined Brad had used to the stolen gun to rob the convenience store.

I stayed indifferent to save him from the legal system. There was no time to deal with any raw emotions.

CHAPTER 13

Ashley and I began our junior year in Mr. Muir's infamously difficult Algebra 2 class. Mr. Muir was a short stocky man. His nickname was Marsh Mouth Muir. He was accustomed to smoking cigarettes and drinking black coffee. The teacher was known to pace in between rows of desks, offering his help. Students recoiled from him in disgust.

At the beginning of the class, Mr. Muir wrote a few difficult math problems on the chalkboard. Then he walked to his podium in the corner of the room. I shrank in my seat and avoided eye contact with the teacher. He found a name from the attendance sheet on top of his podium.

"Miss Hayes, solve the first equation," the teacher instructed.

Ashley hesitated to approach the chalkboard. She swiveled in the seat of her desk, stood from her seated position, and inched toward the chalkboard. Her slow pace prolonged the tense situation.

"You can begin, anytime." The teacher proclaimed.

His eyes were cast downward at the list of student names. Then he studied the faces in the classroom. "We're all waiting," the teacher urged. There was sarcasm in his voice.

"I'm thinking," Ashley replied.

Suddenly, she completed the equation and returned to her seat.

"Congratulations. That is correct," the teacher stated.

There was an almost audible sigh of relief from the students. The nervous tension was gone until Mr. Muir called another name. Still, I was filled with pride. It was evident that Ashley could've returned to the private school. She chose to graduate from Glasgow, however.

College was in the forefront of my mind. Every member of the group went on a tour of the University of Delaware.

Toni and I didn't apply to any other colleges. Brad went on the tour just to humor the rest of us. His plan was to move to Florida and enroll in an automotive school. At meetings, he never developed a penchant for hard work.

A familiar rhythm returned to our meetings. Toni devised new exercises every week. Ed kept a record of our progress. Junior year was the most difficult for the fact that I had to prepare for SATs. Plus, my merits had earned me a seat in more advanced classes. The long hours committed to study caused fatigue.

I was already beneath the covers when Toni slipped into my darkened room. She caused the slightest disturbance: a creak in the floorboards, or a click from the latch of the bedroom door. In some manner, I unclosed my eye and observed her shadow gliding into the room. Brad and Ed were roused by her arrival, also.

"Can we change the sleeping arrangement tonight?" She inquired.

In slow motion, Brad and Ed shuffled out of my room with their sleeping bags. Ashley refused to allow them inside the other bedroom. Toni stood silent until they had vanished. Then she closed the door. I observed the door was left unlocked.

"We discussed taking the group in a new direction. I have some ideas," she said.

"Is that the only reason you kicked Brad and Ed out?" I asked.

"I'm tired of peer pressure. You always look at me with sad puppy eyes like I should have sex with you out of pity."

She slid both thumbs inside the waistband of her pajama bottoms. The fabric stretched over her hips. Then she allowed the garment to fall around her feet. My attention was held as if by a spell. She removed each foot, one by one, from the loose garment.

Articles of clothing were discarded on the floor until she stood naked in front of me. I'd never seen her so vulnerable. "Take me," she whispered. Then she lay down on my bed. I removed my clothes, climbed in next to her, and began to explore her body.

Her response to my touch wasn't reciprocal. She stopped all my fondling and pulled away from me. The look in her eyes was fixed and cold. I understood the seriousness of the moment.

"What are you thinking?" She asked.

"I only want to love you," I replied.

"Love me, not the way I make you feel. Embrace the chase."

"How long do I have to run behind you?"

"I have bigger plans than playing house. We can lead the others to believe we had sex, but I'm just not ready."

Toni and I talked until darkness swept over me. I was half-awakened from a dream state by a gentle kiss. "I promise to be your first," she whispered. I drifted back to sleep.

During the week, Toni initiated the first part of her plan. She phoned Christiana Hospital for permission to read to the children in the pediatric department. I gathered various books from my adolescence. Also, I separated some comic books from my collection to be given as gifts.

Toni revealed her plan at the beginning of our next meeting. She would read to the children in a common area. The rest of the group would visit patients unable to gather in the common area. Even Brad couldn't refuse an effort to bring happiness to unwell children.

The following day, we rode to the hospital in Ashley's car. Toni introduced herself to someone at the information desk. Another employee escorted everybody to the pediatric department. We were directed to wait in a large playroom.

I watched as children filled the playroom. One boy wore a baseball cap to conceal his chemo-induced hair loss. A nurse pushed one girl in a wheelchair. Casually, we left Toni in the playroom.

We went to visit disabled patients. I met a young boy in traction due to a car accident. I experienced a heartwarming feeling each time a smile spread across a child's face. Patients who are not awake received a gift to discover later.

Eventually, I left a notice with staff at the nurses' station: everyone should meet in the cafeteria. Toni was still reading to the children. I roamed the halls of the hospital, witnessing patients suffer. Doctors and nurses worked hard to ease their suffering. The care and remedies they delivered were miraculous.

Ashley and Ed were seated inside the cafeteria already. Ashley was seated with paramedics on a break from emergency calls. Ed wasn't in the company of other people. He ate a meal of food available in the cafeteria. I joined him at the table.

"Where's Brad?" I asked.

"Haven't seen him lately," he answered.

So I went to find him. I wandered without aim, peering into every room along my route. He was with a patient in the ICU.

I entered the room in a casual manner to avoid suspicion. The situation was cause for alarm. Brad had disconnected an oxygen tube from the source of the outflow. He had stuffed a joint inside the tube, lit the joint, and supplied smoke to the patient via the tube. My sudden appearance didn't stop his activity.

"You're going to get us in trouble!" I whispered.

"He's in a coma. No one has checked on him in over an hour," he replied.

I removed the joint from the plastic tubing. Then I snuffed it out. A fusion of adrenaline and anger fueled my actions. The odor of marijuana inside the small room was pungent. I was worried I might get caught, holding the evidence. The elderly man bolted upright in his hospital bed.

"Pudding!" He yelled.

"I'll get the nurse for you, sir," I told him.

"I need chocolate pudding," he continued.

The patient continued to yell as we ran away. We met the others in the cafeteria and left the hospital.

We continued charitable acts throughout the school year. Ashley was motivated to organize fundraisers. Contributions went towards school intramurals.

Toni deserved a special act of kindness. I invited her to an early dinner at my house. The main course was shrimp scampi with linguine noodles. We engaged in casual conversation during the meal.

"You're a better cook than I'd imagined," she said.

"I shared my dream with you, and you made it a reality. You deserve this and more," I replied.

We reminisced about events absent from my thoughts for some time. Her memory was impressive. She mentioned times we had spoken only a word or two. It was a bothersome task, but dinnerware needed to be cleared from the table. Also, desert needed some final preparations.

Earlier, I baked two batches of fudge brownies. The first tray was laced with Afgan hash purchased from Weedeater. I told Toni that half the brownies were laced with hash.

"Is that your idea of an edible aphrodisiac? Are you trying to take advantage of me?" She asked.

"I've tried everything else," I responded.

"Just keep trying. I'd prefer a regular brownie."

A sudden knock at the door brought an abrupt end to our conversation. I went to answer the door after a fudge brownie sundae was delivered to Toni. Ashley stood outside, waiting for someone to answer the door. She entered the dining room, saw the sundae, and demanded one for herself.

The subsequent meeting wasn't productive at all. I offered the leftover brownies to the group. They devoured both trays. Everyone ate at least one brownie laced with hash. Two hours later, our mental concentration was ruined. I savored the last perceptible moment— the sense of sinking into my soft mattress. Darkness encompassed me like a warm, viscous fluid.

CHAPTER 14

At the beginning of summer, Ed suggested the group visit an abandoned rock quarry in Maryland. It was located deep in the forest. Ashley drove on back roads through small towns. Ed gave directions to a hidden trail off the main road. It was overgrown with flora.

The vehicle barely fit between the tree trunks. Sunlight broke through the foliage in small beams. The narrow track of earth disappeared. We abandoned the vehicle a short distance into the forest, unable to advance any further.

I staggered around trees and fallen branches until the trees no longer hindered my sight. A sheer cliff towered around seventy or eighty feet in vertical height. The man-made body of water rested at the foot of the cliff. It was a magnificent shade of aquamarine. The sunlight made the mineral rich water appear to glow. It was a beautiful and serene location.

Everybody swam across the pond to reach the cliff. Climbing on the jagged cliff was dangerous. There was very little foothold in some places. The tranquil water below was disturbed by loose rocks. I felt diminished by the exertion.

At length, everybody reached the summit. We held hands to jump from the ledge together. A few individuals were too leery for that to occur, however. I didn't trust Brad wouldn't push me over the edge.

One by one, we summoned the courage to jump from the craggy ledge. The duration of the fall was longer in my mind. The forceful impact with the water below stung the bottoms of my feet. I swam fast to avoid a collision with the next person to jump.

Toni and Ashley stretched blankets over a large boulder after their jump from the cliff. The boulder was large enough to protrude into the pond. They sunbathed while the rest of us continued to leap from the cliff.

This excursion was the last time we were all together in one location. Brad announced he was no longer in academic jeopardy. Ed asked him to reconsider, but he was determined to leave the group. Toni caught the relieved expression on my face.

The individuals that remained took several trips to the beach over the course of summer. Ashley suggested we rent a beach house after we graduated from high school.

We visited a realtor in Rehoboth, Delaware. I placated her at first. The properties she selected were too expensive. "I'll tell my dad it's a graduation present," she insisted. I didn't want to think about graduation yet.

Senior year was the last chance to appreciate the kinship between classmates. I only needed a few more credits to graduate. My last class ended before lunch. Toni and I had the same schedule. We spent a considerable amount of time together: studying, preparing for the prom, and helping others. We organized a food drive and collected donations for Goodwill.

One morning, I passed a car full of teens in the student parking lot. The rear window came down and smoked billowed out into the open air. "Wake and bake!" Brad shouted. His arm extended out of the window to offer whatever drug he was smoking. I detected the scent of marijuana in the air. The other people in the car had drugs too. I suspected Brad had supplied them with drugs. I refused to accept his offer and walked to class.

Later, it became apparent he was a drug dealer. I saw him make transactions on school property. More and more students used drugs at school. The situation caused the school administration to install video cameras and hire security guards.

Brad moved to Florida before the end of classes. Ed told me about Brad's departure. We were at the tuxedo rental shop.

Toni and Ashley shopped for dresses on more than one occasion. Toni selected a simple black dress. It was a floor-length evening gown. I bought a purple orchid corsage for her wrist.

We took pictures at my house. The atmosphere was peculiar. She insisted we go for a drive before the others arrived in a rented limousine. Her sullen mood indicated this wasn't a matter of little importance.

Questions without answers filled my mind as I was transported through large iron gates. She navigated narrow roads with rows of tombstones on either side. Then she parked her vehicle without a word.

The silence remained unbroken as I followed her to a burial plot. Her eyes filled with tears. Tears fomented by the sight of a large marble headstone. Witnessing her agony made my heart hurt.

"I want you to meet someone, Mom," she began.

"You might remember him. This is Ben."

"I wanted to thank you—you saved me from drowning," I said.

I endeavored to evoke a memory of the unseen figure. Toni pointed to a small headstone beside her mother's. Tears fell, one by one, from her face to the soft ground.

"Maria is my little sister," she continued.

"Do you mind telling me what happened?"

"My mom died during labor. I was told it was placenta previa."

"That's what you went through all those years ago. You shouldn't have to know so much pain at such a young age."

"I've spent so many days here: anniversaries, holidays, and birthdays. I grew up in this place."

She took my hand and placed an engagement ring in the center of my palm. I studied the ring, feeling its weight. It felt out of place. Toni choked on emotions as they burst through the damaged levee inside her.

"It was my mother's engagement ring," she sobbed.

"Your mother thought I was a weirdo. Are you sure we have her blessing?" I asked. "Tell me, it's only a matter of time."

"Of course."

I couldn't bear the anguished expression on her face any longer. The entire atmosphere of mourning threatened to overpower my senses. I left her side, but there was no solace to be found. A new regard for Toni mingled with my existing feelings. I hoped the festivities ahead would influence the somber atmosphere around us.

A limo full of friends and classmates arrived at my house. More photos were taken before we departed for the prom. A chauffeur drove our group to a banquet hall on the college campus. The gala was a very formal location.

There was a buffet of food served from silver salvers. The banquet was accompanied by a dance. The dance took place in a ballroom filled with streamers and balloons matching our school colors. The limo provided transportation to my house after the formal affair.

Everybody changed into costumes for a fantasy themed after-party at Glascow High. Ashley dressed as a princess, and her date wore a prince costume. Ed and his date wore robot costumes. Toni and I were the fairy duo from Shakespeare's *A Midsummer Night's Dream*. We took inspiration for King Oberon and Queen Titania from costumes in the classic film.

The high school had games of chance, including: skee ball, ring toss, and throwing darts. A band took requests while colored lights engulfed people on the gym floor. Toni gave me a reassuring smile as we danced to an upbeat tune. We didn't stay long after Ashley was announced prom queen.

The plan was to spend the following day in Atlantic City, New Jersey. At least half of the group fell asleep during the ride. None of the girls wanted to go further than an awkward embrace. So they decided to rent a hotel room for themselves.

On graduation day, both my parents were available to witness me in my cap and gown. The ceremony was held inside the auditorium on the college campus. Students walked across the stage, shook the principal's hand, and took their diploma. I applauded louder whenever someone from the study group received their diploma.

Toni gave her valedictorian speech after the parade of students. She spoke for over twenty minutes. The crowd was energized by her words. Her speech was filled with: milestones from the past, hopes for the future, and unmitigated standards of excellence.

Later, students and their families lingered outside the auditorium. My mother ran over and threw her arms around me. Tears streamed from her eyes. "I'm so proud," she said. My father kept his distance. He had the audacity to bring his new family.

My father introduced me to his second wife and her daughter. To be honest, I preferred the company of the young college student over his second wife. He blindsided me with news of a graduation party at his house.

Toni and I were only at his house for a very short duration. We anticipated the party at Ashley's house would be much more fun. Besides, I wasn't familiar with most of my father's guests. There were only a few relatives from his side of the family. Most of the guests were his friends and neighbors.

Eventually, I waved goodbye to the people gathered in my father's backyard. I felt as though it was an inconvenience for his guests to return the gesture. He walked with us to Toni's vehicle.

My brother was in the middle of the street with his dirt bike idling. He revved the engine and tore down the street at a high rate of speed. I anticipated his return, assuming he would allow me to ride his bike.

"Can I ride?" I asked him.

"No," my father intervened.

"That's for your brother. Just like the party was for you."

"Don't be a dick," I said.

The look on my brother's face was priceless. I didn't give the conversation much thought. My father didn't react right away. Toni got behind the wheel of her vehicle and closed the door. At this instant, my father placed his hand on my shoulder and tightened his grip. This was his opportunity to have the final word.

"I'll put you on your ass if you ever call me a dick again," he whispered.

Ashley's house was overrun with people. The house was situated on 4.8 acres. Someone with a discerning eye had decorated the interior. There was a huge pool with a waterfall and grotto area in the backyard. Horses lived in a small stable. People rode one horse around the property. I felt the sting of class inferiority.

At dusk, a bonfire was started in a fire pit near the pool. Guests toasted marshmallows and made s'mores. The pinnacle of the evening came when Ashley's father presented keys to a rental property. A large cake and an assortment of ice cream made it difficult to choose one flavor.

Ashley scampered through the crowd, dangling her shiny keys in the faces of her guests. Her only grievance was that nobody brought marijuana to her party. The notion caused her to question the availability of marijuana at the beach.

"How are we going to score over the summer?" She asked.

"I volunteer to take the road trip," I offered.

"And I'm not taking my Mercedes. The salt air will ruin the paint," she continued.

CHAPTER 15

Ed accompanied me during the drive to the beach. The drive took us very close to Dover Downs Raceway. Toni drove Ashley in her SUV. They left prior to our departure. The drugs were transported to the beach house in my car. A pound of marijuana and three ounces of magic mushrooms were hidden in my luggage. Our graduation money had been amassed to cover the cost. I lacked genuine concern about the consequences. That was true enough.

We reached the beach house without incident. It looked like a pleasant summer locale. I ran inside to tour the property, leaving Ed unaided with the luggage. Ashley and Toni were on the second floor. I called out to them. There was no response—only indiscernible noises continued to echo from the upstairs.

I entered the living room. The decor had a nautical theme. Floors throughout most of the beach house were beautiful hardwood. Decorative flowers brightened the room. I studied the paintings and nautical maps on the walls.

Ed disturbed my concentration as he forced luggage through the doorway. He was unbalanced by the heavy burden and collided with the front door. I didn't concern myself very much with his struggle. Instead, I continued my tour.

Large sliding glass doors provided a spectacular view of the ocean from the dining room. A wooden deck allowed unobstructed access to the beach. The kitchen was in the back half of the beach house also.

It didn't occur to me to declare a bedroom until it was too late. Ed selected one of the two bedrooms on the first floor. The girls departed earlier, so they could have the master bedroom. I was disappointed Toni didn't choose to share a bed with me, but there was no reason to start the summer with an argument.

The next day, I started my summer job at the video arcade on the boardwalk. All the new employees received one hour of training. The manager described the proper method to: make change for the customers, pick up trash, wipe down machines, sweep, and mop. Uniforms were provided to each new hire. Our only mandatory article of clothing was a T-shirt with the arcade logo.

I ran to the beach house, threw the shirts on my bed, and realized no one else had returned from their first day of work. The weather was too nice to remain indoors. I returned to the boardwalk, traveling the entire length.

Obie's by the Sea was one of the last businesses on the north end of the boardwalk. The restaurant was empty. A crowd of people encircled an older gentleman on the outside deck, however. He was in the middle of a speech.

My intrigue caused the man to halt his speech. He examined me over the rims of his glasses. People in the crowd turned to see who or what was responsible for the interruption. The situation made me feel self-conscious.

"Who are you?" The man asked.

"Ben Pine," I replied.

"I'm the owner. Do you want a job?"

"Yes."

"Come join us."

The owner stood next to a table full of shot glasses. A large bottle of Grand Marnier was delivered to the owner. He filled the glasses with liquor and distributed them to the crowd. I stepped forward with the others to receive a glass. "Are you eighteen?" He asked.

"Yes," I answered.

"Come back to fill out an application. You can be added to the schedule then."

He ended the conversation with a firm handshake. A little of the liquor spilled from the shot glass in my opposite hand. The owner raised his glass and continued his speech.

"Each year, I like to open and close the restaurant with a toast. To a new and profitable business season," he announced.

Later, the taste of Grand Marnier lingered in the back of my throat. It was a bittersweet aftertaste with an orange undertone. I had a positive regard for the liquor and craved more of the flavor. A nearby liquor store sold the brand. I purchased a bottle and drank it at the beach house.

The liquor lowered my inhibitions and loosened my tongue. I introduced an inebriated state through indulgence. Resentment toward Toni roiled inside my mind. I pleaded with her to share my bed. She was reluctant.

"You are broken," I said.

"You are drunk," she replied.

"You are a broken person. You cut people with your sharp edges."

The next morning, I woke with a terrible hangover. This new experience was self-inflicted torture. My stomach quivered and my eyes were sensitive to the light.

Suddenly, Toni's disembodied voice echoed from outside my room.

"You're off to a good start! You're late for work!" She screamed.

The manager of the arcade harassed me about my tardiness. His harsh criticism continued for the duration of the shift. He stood in the middle of the arcade, reprimanding me like I was some kind of degenerate. At the end of the shift, I was summoned to his office.

"I'm not paying you! Keep the shirts and be sure to wear them. I can at least get free advertisement. I don't ever want to see your face around here again!" He ranted.

There was more than a week until my scheduled shifts began at the restaurant. My circle of friends worked most days. So I was alone for long hours.

One day, I ingested magic mushrooms. It was my very first time. Half asleep, lying on the sofa, my stomach started to churn. A pleasant tingle took root in every fiber of my body after the urge to vomit subsided. Distortion in my mind bubbled over and split across reality.

The items inside the beach house took different forms. The wooden coffee table became a chocolate bar, hardwood floors transformed into gingerbread, and tempting candy treats appeared everywhere. I went outside to explore this new delectable world. It resembled a space on the board game Candy Land.

With an unsteady gait, I made a trek across a beach of granular sugar. The sun was formed of two candy orange slices. Clouds of cotton candy floated in the sky. Huge gummy bears roamed the shoreline and frolicked in the ocean. The ocean water had the qualities of a bubbly soda drink.

The water made my skin tingle with a greater intensity. I walked forward into the ocean, cool and refreshing, until some salt water got in my mouth. The taste was disgusting. I evacuated the ocean without delay.

The beach became quicksand under my feet as I moved past the water's reach. It was impossible to orchestrate an escape. Curses and insults were hurled at the gummy bears as they watched me sink.

Eventually, I experienced a lucid moment. It took a few minutes to dig myself out of the sand. Then I stumbled toward the beach house. There was an outdoor shower on the side of the house. I rinsed the sand from my body.

The next few days, I retained adequate presence of mind to avoid another confrontation with Toni. My time was spent sulking in my room. She hovered just outside the open door, waiting for me to address our grudge. I made no effort until she turned to leave.

"Please don't leave," I began. "It's difficult to talk when there's so much disappointment in your eyes."

"I've never seen you drunk," she said.

I clung to the hope that she would forgive me. Her behavior arrested my attention. She shuffled across the floor to the foot of my bed.

"Can I convince you to have a date night with me?" I asked.

Her lips curved upward to form a pleasant smile.

"It might improve your chances. Depends on how fancy the restaurant is. I'd like flowers too. A handwritten apology would be a nice touch," she stated.

She sat beside me on the bed. Her head rested on my shoulder. I breathed her scent. It was a familiar smell that had brought comfort. I traced the infinity sign over the back of her hand. Our unspoken promise to each other.

The following day, I browsed shops along the boardwalk. It was the wrong location to search for flowers and other luxury items. I turned down a side street with less foot traffic. A tattoo shop sidetracked my focus.

The abundance of concept art was impressive, but none of the examples felt right. I chose to get 420 in Roman numerals. It took less than an hour for the artist to tattoo my upper thigh. In that span of time, I decided to search elsewhere.

Afterward, I drove my car to Dover. I bought an outfit that Toni would never have chosen for herself. The dress was red, expensive, and didn't leave much to the imagination. I matched a pair of red stiletto heels with the dress. Two other purchases were made at different stores in the area.

The flower shop provided a dozen red roses. Their color paled in comparison to the dress. The other purchase was a nice suit for myself. Then I selected a restaurant.

It was a short drive down the coast to Ocean City, Maryland. The vague directions given to me over the phone were difficult to recall as I relayed them to Toni. My attention was divided during the drive down the coast. She arched her back against the seat as her foot pressed down on the gas pedal.

Soon, we arrived at the restaurant. I leaped out of the vehicle to intercept the valet, maneuvering to open Toni's door. He accepted the gratuity I offered.

The interior of the restaurant was a contrast of white linen table cloths and stainless steel. Fish swam in aquariums behind decorative portholes on the walls. The clamor of waitstaff and patrons was thunderous. A hostess showed us to our table.

A devilish smile appeared across Toni's face as I pulled out a chair for her. Red matte-finished lipstick coated her lips. Our waitress came to the table for the drink order. "You're supposed to pair white wine with seafood," I blurted out. We both requested water. Then we sat in silence, soaking up the atmosphere.

She continued to study the menu until the waitress returned for our meal order. The conversation was sparse during the meal also. I renewed the thread of conversation after the waitress removed our plates.

"I would like you to wear your mother's ring," I said.

She pushed her chair away from the table and made a swift exit. I had to explain to the waitress that there would be a delay. "Will she be returning?" The waitress asked.

"Yes," I replied.

"I'm only asking because I saw her leave the restaurant." The waitress left with emptied plates.

Finally, Toni returned to the table. She gave my shoulder a light touch to make her proximity known. I felt like my heart had developed an arrhythmia. "You walked out in the middle of my proposal," I told her.

"I went to get my camera," she explained. The camera was entrusted to a random server. They agreed to take numerous photos of the events about to unfold. Without further delay, I positioned myself on one knee.

The events occupied only an instant. She held out her hand. I slid the ring on her finger. People in the restaurant erupted into applause after she agreed to marry me.

Our return to the beach house was quiet. Although the mood was pensive, our body language communicated our closeness. I caressed her knee. She reached over with her right hand, ran it through my hair, and gave my ear a playful tug. It was late when we arrived at the house.

She led the way to my room. We stood in the middle of the floor, staring into each other's eyes. She gripped my tie and pulled me close for a passionate kiss. Her free hand lowered the zipper of my pants in one impatient movement. One button was unfastened and my pants fell to the floor. She yanked down my boxers also.

The only light came from the night sky. Still, she found the tattoo on my thigh. Her fingertips grazed over the area. A twinge of pain made me grimace.

"When did you get a tattoo?" She inquired.

"Yesterday," I answered.

"You can't permanently alter your body without a discussion anymore."

The sound of her heels on the hardwood floor echoed in my ears as she walked out of the room. I was abandoned in the middle of the room with my pants around my ankles.

CHAPTER 16

"What smells so good?"

Toni's question went unanswered for a tense moment. I was busy preparing banana pancakes. She startled me with her sudden approach. Ashley followed close behind. They sauntered into the kitchen, scrutinizing every detail.

"I was thinking about the first breakfast we ate together. So I went to the store and bought a feast," I explained.

The dining room table was laden with an assortment of: cereal, muffins, and fruit. Pitchers of milk and juice chilled in the refrigerator. Also, I had purchased an ornate wooden box of flavored tea and a bag of premium coffee.

"Why are you being so nice?" Toni asked.

"You know," I replied.

She entwined her body with mine and administered a gentle squeeze.

"Can we help with anything?" She offered.

"Would someone get Ed?" I requested.

Ashley volunteered.

"I need to freshen up, anyway."

Toni studied me with strict attentiveness. Then she examined the food a second time.

"I remember the first meal you made for me. Is this meal drug-free?" She asked.

"There are store-bought options if you don't trust my cooking," I replied.

She noticed my mug of tea on a nearby counter. The banana nut muffin flavored tea was the best I had ever tasted. She readied a mug for herself. I stopped her before she removed the tea kettle from the stove top. "Wait!" I urged. Her instinct was to lift the lid of the teakettle. I had strained the magic mushrooms from the boiling water with a slotted spoon already.

"What's wrong with the water?" She inquired.

"I boiled shrooms in it," I explained.

"Have you thought about the possibility that your perception of reality is being tainted by drugs?"

"Please, don't make me have a bad trip."

I took possession of the mug and headed toward my bedroom. Leaning against the closed door, it felt like everything was about to evacuate my stomach. I forced the contents of my stomach down with two hard swallows. Beads of perspiration formed on my brow. It was hard to concentrate while my brain disputed reality.

I entered further into the room. It was my intention to roll myself a joint. Remembering the location of certain items was a difficult task. The walls came to life, breathing in and exhaling out. The door swelled like a bubble or balloon. It burst when a hard knock was delivered to the opposite side. I was frightened by the commotion.

"Not right now!" I Yelled.

"I'm coming in." Toni insisted.

The door opened, and she entered the room. This action created a ripple effect. I saw the same action repeated over and over. A trail was formed by the repeated process.

"What are you doing?" She asked.

Her eyes stared straight into mine.

"I want to smoke something," I said.

She completed a scavenger hunt for the necessary items, sat on the edge of my bed, and rolled a joint.

"What's my name?" She continued.

"Don't patronize me," I complained.

"I don't look like: The Oracle at Delphi, Mona Lisa, or Venus."

I thought about the famous paintings. Each scene represented a unique style from a different period. I attempted to recall the name of each artist. Toni was always the muse.

"What are you seeing?" She inquired.

"Trails of movement," I explained.

"Come back out to the kitchen. We can smoke out there."

She convinced me to go against my own instincts. It was impossible to resist her, even if such a thought entered my mind. Indeed, the undeniable truth was she made everything in life better. I finished my tea and followed her out of the room.

Ashley and Ed enjoyed their breakfast in the dining room. We sat and smoked with them. Ashley pointed at me with her fork. "This is delish," she began. "Toni told me about your tattoo."

"We should all get one," Ed announced.

"Can you get more of this tea?" Ashley asked.

"Did you use the water in the teakettle?" I implored.

"Of course I did. The lavender flavor is delish," she replied.

Ashley repeated the word lavender over and over.

"You seem weirded out, Ashley."

Toni stated, "What does that mean?

"Say that again?" She requested.

"Weirded out. Outside your normal state."

"You are so smart, you're dumb."

"Why does it feel like I ate a box of crayons?" Ed inquired.

"Your coffee and Ashley's tea was made with shroom water. Boiling the mushrooms might have had a more potion effect," I explained.

This predicament exemplified the entire summer. Each individual captivated by a unique, twirling dance shared between memory and imagination. Only an extraordinary act of will could bring us back to our former selves. Toni was the only exception.

She was a guardian angel. A guide to illuminate the path on this plane of existence. She encouraged me to be my best self, even though I'd chosen to indulge in vice.

CHAPTER 17

All of my available money was spent in less than two weeks. The biggest expenditure was my date night with Toni. Other expenses included: food, alcohol, and gas for my car. The job at the restaurant didn't start soon enough. Without any source of income, I decided to ask my family for money.

The drive to Newark didn't take a considerable amount of time. Soon, I arrived at my mother's house. The absence of occupants wasn't as jarring as the condition of the property. My childhood home had suffered a slow ruin over the years.

Filth defiled the surrounding area. Trash littered the ground. The lawn wasn't maintained with the devotion my father bore. Dark spots left by oil stained the driveway. Leaves were left to decay on the roof and inside the rain gutters.

Inside the house, I studied every detail with a measure of melancholy. The furniture was chipped along the edges, no longer pristine. The stench of smoke and tar permeated the environment. The walls were dingy. A putrid smell crept out of the kitchen.

The linoleum floor felt spongy underneath my shoes. Cabinets were covered with black soot from burnt meals. The stove was covered with grease. Dirty dishes were piled high in the sink. An area around the dishwasher was warped and coated with black mold. I remembered the incident that caused the damage.

At the time, my mother was under the influence of an unknown substance. She had absentmindedly filled the dishwasher with too much detergent. The machine was left unattended after my mother deserted the house. My attention had been drawn away from a video game by the faint splash of water. Bubbles had filled the kitchen floor. Water had traveled down the wall in one section of the basement.

The unpleasant smell forced me out of the kitchen. I found a phone in another room and placed a call to my father's house. My stepmother's daughter answered the call. She wanted permission to visit the beach house.

"I'll have to run that by my friends," I told her.

"The best time to catch your dad is at dinner," she explained.

"Can you tell your mother to expect me?"

Finally, I completed my tour of the house. Then I loaded some essential items into my car. It was important to be punctual for dinner at my father's house. So I drove to his house at a high rate of speed.

I scrutinized the entire neighborhood. There were no sidewalks for pedestrians. This would indicate any interaction between neighbors was uncommon. Each dwelling was isolated from the others.

My stepmother greeted me with an overdone friendliness. Then she cast her gaze downward. Wearing shoes inside the house earned me an admonishment. This house was kept clean with meticulous detail. I returned to the foyer, removed my shoes, and placed them by the door. Then I was shown my place at the table.

Dinner was served when my father took his seat. My stepmother was steadfast in her preparations. The meal was served on fine china. She poured water into crystal glasses. No one spoke until I broke the silence.

"What is that?" I asked.

"A vacuum unit," my father began.

"There is one in almost every room. The dirt travels to a central bin in the basement."

The meal continued without further interruption. My stepmother cleared the table after everyone had finished the meal.

"I thought you were spending the summer at the beach," my father stated.

"Things are more expensive than I expected," I replied.

"Aren't you working?"

"I start in a few days. I could use some money to hold me over."

"I want you to behave like a responsible young adult while you're at the beach. I'm proud of you."

He escorted me outside after my visit. A crisp hundred-dollar bill was removed from his wallet. I accepted the money and gave him a hug.

"How is your car running?" He asked.

"Fine," I began. "It should get me back and forth when classes start."

"How much will your job cover? Do I need to fill out any paperwork?

Your stepsister is starting college too."

"Does that mean you're not helping me at all?"

"No, I won't be able to help you. You'll have to apply for loans to cover the cost."

"That's a real dick move."

My father landed a strong right hook on my chin. I'd never been hit that hard in my life. The two points of my lower jaw stabbed into the base of my skull. My entire body stiffened like a starched shirt. The force of the impact propelled me backward. Everything went to black. The length of time I had been unconscious remained a mystery.

Eventually, I regained consciousness. My stepmother was there when I open my eyes. I gathered myself off the street.

"I think you should leave now. We don't want another incident," she stated.

I decided to return to my mother's house before leaving Newark. She had returned home. We argued whether or not a call should be placed to the police. I didn't want to delay my return to the beach any longer.

Toni noticed the bruise on my face straightaway. I told her about the incident and how my father had persuaded me to attend the University of Delaware. He had taken me to numerous college football games when I was younger. My head was filled with dreams of playing football on that same field one day. I thought my father worked at the college with the sole purpose of getting a deduction. She promised to help ensure my attendance at the college.

Those concerns could be sorted out later. I was in the mood to drink. A walk to the liquor store allowed time to convince myself that my plan was still possible. My father's money paid for an ample amount of alcohol.

The next few days, I drank a profuse amount of alcohol. The days spent more drunk than sober were a blur. I was glad Toni had chosen to sleep in a different bed. My bed felt too soft and the room started to spin. I woke on the floor in a pool of my own vomit. It was difficult to remember the day of the week. I managed to report to work sober, however.

My first day at the restaurant was a challenge. I was thrown into the dishwasher position without any training. My duties consisted of: washing dishes, taking trash to the dumpster, and collecting empty beer bottles in matching empty cases. At the end of my shift, I reeked of sweat, hot garbage, and alcohol. The spray from the dishwashing machine soaked me from head to toe.

Obie's by the Sea was a popular destination. The food was better than typical platters of deep-fried seafood served elsewhere. Employees arrived for work around 9:00 a.m. Everyone contributed their effort to open the restaurant, but a shift manager noticed my exemplary work ethic.

I was ordered to clear tables during service. In return, the waitstaff relinquished 20% of their tips. At the end of the shift, I received cash. It made the extra work worthwhile.

Over time, I developed a rapport with the bartenders. We reached an agreement that was mutually beneficial. I would tip the bartenders twenty dollars and they gave me free drinks. Drinks that were not quite right for customers or left over from a proper drink. I spent hours at the bar after my shift.

One evening, I drank like a thirsty sailor at the bar. The hot sun was replaced by a full moon. I left the restaurant. Stars illuminated one by one during my stroll to the beach house. The salt air had a renewing effect on the state of my mind.

I staggered inside the beach house, managed to remove all my clothes, and departed through the sliding glass door. My companions followed me out to the shoreline. Nothing they said prevented me from diving into the ocean water. I struggled to tread water.

Suddenly, a rip current dragged me out to sea. I lost sight of my companions as I dipped underneath the waves. I was able to breach the surface again. Toni emitted one bloodcurdling scream after another. Somehow, she swam into the current and brought me back to shore. I was cradled in her arms, my naked body sprawled out on the beach.

"I love you—Ben, I love you," she repeated.

"Everyone heard you… I have witnesses," I whispered.

Toni pushed me away. She stormed off the beach, leaving me on the sand. The others followed her inside.

CHAPTER 18

Ashley invited people from her place of employment to a party at the beach house. There were always random strangers in the house afterward. People who were: drunk, high, out of control, some combination, or all of the above. Parties grew so large they spilled out onto the beach at times.

There was one silver lining. Toni and I slept in the same bed. Ashley was not shy about how many random guys spent the night. So Toni was forced to find other arrangements.

Plenty of guys tried to seduce Toni too. I felt compelled to warn one fellow after he groped her. He was very intoxicated. Ashley pulled him away before a violent altercation began between us.

"Why don't we go upstairs?" She suggested.

And what I thought was that I had to somehow remain indifferent. The impulse within my heart refused to be ignored, however. I surrendered to my curiosity and crept up the stairs. Listening outside the master bedroom door I heard a male voice. He made a raunchy comment. Ashley and Toni toyed with him and laughed at his frustration. He pleaded for them to join him in a threesome.

His comments sent me over the edge. No rationale was formed in my mind as profane instincts took hold. The girls were startled as I burst into the room. The drunk remained oblivious until I collided with him. My momentum sent us both down on the floor. Ashley screamed in protest of my actions. I flashed an angry glance in her direction. The rage in my eyes caused her to flinch.

At that moment, I felt the initial surge of adrenaline. My hands were set loose, finding his face. His face was pressed hard against the floor. I let my hand slide off his cheek and dropped my elbow onto his temple region with all my strength. His body went limp straight-away. Adrenaline overwhelmed my senses.

I couldn't stop myself from further action. His limp body was dragged from the room by a pant leg. Many people were disturbed by the site of a lifeless body being dragged down the stairs. I pulled him through a crowd of young people.

Suddenly, he regained consciousness. I felt uneasy in the crowd. He kicked free from my grasp and collected himself off the floor. His lead hand snapped inches in front of my face. The other swung in a wide arc behind the lead jab. I stepped sideways to avoid the wild haymaker, pivoting behind him. The opportunity to slide my arms underneath his was there. So I placed him in a full Nelson hold.

The leverage I had allowed me to force him toward the rear exit. I walked with short careful steps through the open glass door. He was shoved outside and onto the sand below the deck. There was an energized flash of activity as he regained his stance. I moved with caution onto the uneven beach.

Without warning, another young man came to aid the irate drunk. He charged like a rampant bull and tackled me. We both came down hard on the sand. The drunk dove into the struggle. He smacked me in the face with a handful of sand. Sand was ground into my face before I could stop him.

Eventually, I was able to grip two of his fingers. He shouted in pain as I bent his fingers in an awkward direction. The second assail-ant landed repeated strikes to my body and face. I managed to elbow him in the face. The drunk was ready to bite my arm. I saw him bare his teeth and released his fingers.

A crowd gathered to observe as we scrambled back to our feet. I doubted the mob would allow me to escape the fray. The drunk lunged in my direction first. I kicked him with my right leg. The heel of my foot sank into his stomach. He fell to one knee. I rushed to ambush him, but the other combatant prevented me.

I was struck upon the temple by a strong right hook. White lights flashed before my eyes. The second assailant avoided my coun-terattack. Also, the drunk returned to his feet. I circled the beach, battling to regain my equilibrium.

Leaping through the air, I fell upon the drunk. We struggled for position. I mounted his torso and punched with both fists like an unhinged maniac. I was placed in a chokehold from behind and dragged away. I delivered blows hard and fast with my elbows until the grip around my neck loosened.

My palms overlapped at the nape of the second assailant's neck. His head recoiled from the vicious impact of my forehead against his face. Blood sprayed from his nose. He crumbled onto the sand. A kick to his head ensured he was out of the fight. I surveyed the crowd afterward.

Some people gasped at the brutality of my actions while others erupted with a congratulatory applause and cheers. I wasn't concerned with those strangers. My intention was to find Toni's familiar face. I found her in the midst of the crowd. She shook her head with disapproval, but I delivered one additional strike to render the drunk unconscious.

Ashley stepped into the clearance as the crowd dispersed from the scene. Her gaze averted mine. "Can you put them in Toni's GMC?" She asked. I carried the two young men to her vehicle with help from Ed. Ashley and Toni left without any further dialogue. They drove off into the night.

I went to clear the beach house of people. People were herded outside after the loud music was off. "Get out!" I shouted. "Everybody get out!" The interior was emptied—only Ed remained inside the house with me.

"Where did that come from?" He asked.

"Don't talk to me right now," I answered. "I didn't see you rushing to intervene."

I had a severe headache. A soak in the Jacuzzi tub would hasten my recovery. So I enjoyed a long soak before Ashley and Toni returned to the beach house. I assumed Toni wouldn't want to spend the night in my bed.

Later, Ashley barged into my room. "Did you use my tub?" She yelled.

"Yeah," I replied.

"Clean it out, next time. There was hair and filth everywhere. You fucking animal!"

After she stormed out of the room, I turned off the lights and prepared for sleep. My clothes were a source of irritation. Even the soft bedsheets caused an annoyance to my sore body. I felt every nick and scrape the sand left on my skin. My eyelids hurt.

I was on the verge of sleep when a feminine silhouette entered through the doorway. A moonbeam illuminated the shadow figure as she passed a window. Toni glared at me with pursed lips and flared nostrils from the side of my bed. She undressed and climbed into the bed.

The peak of the season was hot and humid. Perspiration on our skin glistened when the intermittent twilight moonbeam poured into the room. One arm draped over my torso. She moved closer and nuzzled my neck. Our skin clung together. The pull toward her was continuous as if I couldn't be close enough.

"Take me," she whispered.

I pressed myself between her thighs. She helped guide me inside with her hands. Every touch was tender and affectionate. The intimacy we shared was awkward, however. She gasped and bolted upright, clutching tight enough for her nails to pierce the skin on my back.

"Don't move," she ordered.

She drew her body apart from mine. I felt an explosion of intense pleasure as she slipped away. Our first sexual encounter was brief and awkward. We stayed awake all night, making love to each other. The intimacy felt more natural, as our bodies moved in unison.

CHAPTER 19

A few more trips to Newark were necessary. The drugs didn't last for the entire summer. Also, we had to register for classes. Ashley and Ed were accepted to out-of-state colleges. Knowing our time together was limited weighed upon me. My friends filled the void created by my broken home. I felt the urge to visit my mother again.

A stranger greeted me at the door. She welcomed me inside. There was an entire family in my house. My mother broke the bad news, explaining how she had lost the house. She could no longer keep up with the payments. My childhood home was no longer possessed by my family. The new family needed to move before the sale could be finalized. They were kind enough to compromise with my mother. She was afforded added time to find a new place to live. These revelations killed the vibe at the beach house.

I thought the summer would end with one wild party after another. That wasn't the case, however. The parties ceased and the beach house was kept as clean as possible. We spent plenty of time together, but kept our work schedule. We survived off of whatever food could be brought home from our jobs. There were some late-night strolls to the corner store for Kraft mac and cheese too.

Ashley and Ed struggled to control their emotions as they departed the beach house. Toni and I spent the final days together. With two days left, I drove to Maryland to purchase fireworks. We watched fireworks from the shore after a special dinner.

One morning, we surrendered the keys to the rental property. Toni returned home, but I wanted to stay behind. The restaurant was closing for the off-season. I expected a party and free alcohol.

It was the only other time I saw the owner. He made his final speech and distributed free shots of Grand Marnier to employees. In fact, I was able to drink for free the entire time. It took a few hours to prepare the restaurant for the long winter months.

In the end, I was too drunk to drive. A bartender offered to let me sleep it off at his rental property. He was able to sneak a case of beer out to his car. We drank beer until sunrise.

Still, I was able to reach Newark before sundown. I dreaded my return. My room was no longer mine. The new owners occupied that room. Their children stayed in my brother's old room. I slept on a couch in the basement.

There were two weeks of summer break left. In two weeks, classes began at Delaware Technical Community College or Dell-Tech. I was told I could transfer to University of Delaware if my grades were exemplary. I wanted that big college campus experience.

In the meanwhile, it was necessary to find a job. My first application was submitted at Ripe Tomatoes. I had found memories of Main Street on Saturday night. The manager called me to schedule an interview. He looked to be a little older than me. I was given a sample container during the interview.

"We need a urine sample," he stated.

"Really!?" I replied.

"We can't have you mowing down children while you drive through neighborhoods."

I was certain my sample would test positive for drugs. My brain was wracked to manufacture an excuse. "I don't have to go at the present time," I explained.

"We have soda or water," he answered.

The manager studied my face for a moment. Then he stretched his arm across the desk and motioned for me to return the container. "Relax. We don't hire squares," he said.

"Are you hiring me?" I inquired.

"There is a thirty-day probation. The full-time position is available if you're cool. The owner has the final word."

My probation was spent working alongside the owner. His name was Vincent Marino. He had served as a Marine during the Vietnam War. Sometimes, he had difficulties with personal demons. He spent much of the day behind the locked door of his office.

There weren't many deliveries throughout the early shift. Students hadn't returned to campus in large numbers yet. The owner was surprised when someone requested me to deliver their pizza. I realized who had requested me by name straightaway.

Toni answered the door after I arrived at her dorm room. She invited me inside to talk. We had conversed via the phone, but this was our first encounter in days. I wanted to determine when we might spend more time together.

"I'm not settled into a routine yet," she said.

"Can I sleep here?" I asked.

CHAPTER 20

Pain roused me from an uneasy slumber. Mind-numbing pain had crept its way inside my brain; it had traversed a network of nerve endings, originating in my right thigh. I resolved to rid myself of the source of irritation.

By means of quick observation, I discovered Toni's knee positioned in a manner difficult to dislodge without a disturbance to her sleep. Her hot breath tormented my nostrils. My patient sufferance succumbed to the physical torment. The bed in her dorm room was too small for two adults, and my back was pressed against the wall. I proceeded to use a gentle hand on the knee embedded in my thigh.

A satisfied sigh of triumph escaped my lips. The muscles in my thigh quivered with a blissful sense of relief. I folded my arms across my chest and feigned an innocent sleep as Toni changed her position. She twisted her body and a forearm came to rest upon my face. Her arm slid down to the crook of my neck. She remained asleep, however. Her deep rhythmic breathing resumed and rivaled her roommates'. I didn't dare wake them. They would certainly force me to return to the couch.

The unavoidable moment presented itself when the alarm began to chime. Toni pulled me out of the bed and pushed me out of the room. She gathered my clothes and shoved them into my expectant arms. Then the door was closed with a demonstrative slam.

There was no one present to witness me get dressed. The hordes of students weren't wandering the campus yet. My car waited in an inconspicuous parking space. I climbed into the driver's seat and rubbed the cramp in my right thigh.

I drove through downtown Newark. The morning rush hour traffic congested the streets. The college campus was returning to life.

A sense of gloom pierced my heart as I drove toward my childhood home.

Sunlight filtered through cumulus clouds. Shadows danced across the landscape of my destination. As I entered the house, my mother arose from a sofa in the living room. She was surrounded by household items and cardboard boxes.

"Have you found a place to live?" I inquired.

"I put a down payment on a trailer in Waterford," she replied.

"Can I help?" I offered.

My every movement was under close scrutiny. None of my decisions were correct. I rolled a crystal candleholder in newspaper. My mother mentioned she had the original box.

I placed an item inside a moving box, and she removed it. "I only want to help," I said.

"Just leave me alone now," she demanded. The item in her hand was given a strong regard. It may have invoked some cherished memory. Her eyes shut. One tear escaped and rolled down her cheek. I didn't care to watch my mother weep any longer.

There wasn't much to pack in my old room. Someone had taken my clothes and placed them in large garbage bags. The walls had already been painted over. It struck me that some of my things were missing.

A phone call from my boss interrupted my thoughts. Vince requested my presence at the pizzeria. So I showered and changed clothes. Then I went to my place of employment.

I arrived at Ripe Tomatoes around noon. The employees were busy preparing orders for the lunch rush. Vince stopped his supervision and brought me into his office. "I need you to go over your schedule with Ryan. Classes are back in session, and I need all-hands-on-deck. Why don't you make yourself a pizza and wait for Ryan? What's your favorite topping?" He said.

"Pepperoni," I answered.

"I'll remember that. Go ahead."

Vince was actually testing my ability to make a pizza.

He observed my technique from a distance, watching with a knowledgeable appreciation as I kneaded a ball of dough. Afterward, I stretched the ball into a wide circle.

"Stop!" Vince insisted.

He washed his hands with an energetic motion. Then he positioned himself at my side. I allowed him to take over. He pounded the dough with his fist.

"You have to get all that air out," he instructed.

Soon, the dough was flattened into a disk. He threw the disc toward the ceiling. My eyes grew with amazement. He caught the disc with both fists, stretching and turning the disc in one motion. Next, he began a circus-like performance. The disc flew into the air over and over. It traveled around his back and over his shoulder. The spinning object doubled in size. His acrobatic performance was akin to a skilled gymnast.

I was in a trance, watching his exhibition of skill. His technique for adding sauce and toppings resembled a masterful painter. The pizza was placed on a moving conveyor and entered the oven. He turned toward me and clapped his hands together. A fine cloud of flour dispersed into the air. He spoke a phrase in Italian. Afterward, he disappeared like a magician from the stage.

The pizzeria was small. I ate my pizza at the only available seating. Employees arrived to relieve the first shift. Ryan gave me a sideway glance as he entered the shop.

Ryan and the other employees were sending out strange vibes. They had nicknamed me the FNG.

The owner departed while I finish my pizza. Ryan occupied the office in his absence. He listened to a rock station on a portable radio. The loud music was audible throughout the shop. He never bothered to lower the volume during our conversation.

"Vincent wants to schedule you during peak hours," he began.

"That's why I'm here on my day off," I interrupted.

"If I don't want to work with you, you won't be on the schedule. Don't go over my head. Follow the chain of command. Come to me with any concerns," he continued.

"Okay, I get it," I told him.

"I've already made the schedule for next week. Do you want to work tonight?" He offered.

"Sure," I answered.

Ryan only sent me on deliveries in residential areas. The deliveries took more time, but I assumed the tips were better. College students weren't known to give large tips.

CHAPTER 21

Returning to Toni's dorm room was a bad decision. Her roommate, Linda Noble, didn't hesitate to express her feelings of disapproval. She took a long look into my eyes and smiled in a pretentious manner that said, *we won't ever be close, but feel free to pretend.* Her arms were folded across her chest.

"Do you want me to leave?" I asked.

"This isn't some flophouse," she responded.

"He's not going anywhere," Toni interjected.

Toni clutched me and pulled me down onto her bed. We tumbled in a passionate lover's embrace. Desire coursed through my body like electricity. She pinned me down hard against the mattress. Her forearms came to rest on my chest. Long strands of her raven hair danced across my face and tickled the skin.

"I sleep so well with you here," she said.

"Your roommate isn't wrong. I don't belong here. It feels like I don't belong anywhere," I admitted.

"It's only temporary. Your mom will find a place soon."

"She's moving to a trailer park. It doesn't seem like she wants me around. She would rather I lived with my father."

"Mommy and Daddy issues," Linda interrupted. "You feel abandoned. How fascinating."

Time dragged on for the few remaining hours. Every moment that passed intensified my anxiety. Linda listened to music through the headphones of her Discman. She cupped the headphones and swayed with enthusiasm.

Toni decided to examine her newly acquired textbooks. Our bodies overlapped as we laid on the tiny bed.

Suddenly, Linda began singing along with the music. Her voice was not melodic or soothing. She only wanted to prove her presence filled the room more than mine. Everything about her reminded me of someone I'd been acquainted with during high school: cheerleader, rich family, and a sense of entitlement.

"How long has it been since you smoked?" Toni whispered.

"A few days," I replied.

"How are you doing?"

"Fine. Not being able to contact my guy is the real torment. I'm afraid to go by his place. If he did get arrested, the police might have his place under surveillance."

"What are you going to do?"

"I'd like to find out what happened."

"It would be best to make this the last sleepover for a while."

I waited for Toni to say something else. She only frowned and gave me a sympathetic look. I glanced at Linda. She stared back with the look of a person in need of a demonic exorcism. Her continued scrutiny made me feel foolish.

Soon, Toni was prepared for sleep. Lying beside each other in bed, she whispered across her pillow. "I love falling asleep with you. The sound of your breathing is my favorite lullaby."

"Sweet dreams," I said.

"Sweet dreams, Ben."

The subsequent sleep was far from sweet. The shame pooled around me like a viscous fluid. I felt Linda's eyes, watching with fascinated disgust. A tightness crept into my chest. It spread like uneven cracks through ice under an enormous weight.

I awoke gasping for air. Toni's elbow jutted into my diaphragm. I crawled out of my predicament like a larva digging through the earth. I inched toward the door at a less than desirable speed. Sneaking out was for the best, though.

Stars were still visible in the sky. I felt sluggish from the lack of sleep. So I went to sleep on the couch in the basement. The sun was out when foot traffic on the flooring above disturbed my nap.

The two young boys scrambled to get ready for school. Their mother shouted instructions. Loud impacts indicated the heavy work boots worn by their father. Every sound constituted an indignation. The grievance with the family was a total fabrication on my part. A joyous activity was brought to my soul after I believed the family had gone.

Then I heard the loud whistle of the teakettle.

I went upstairs to investigate the noise. The mother of the two boys, Emily, had made a cup of coffee. She enjoyed her coffee at the dining table. I made something to eat and sat across from her at the table. She was the first to speak. I didn't meet Emily's eyes when she spoke.

"Do you drink coffee?" She asked.

"I don't want any coffee," I answered.

A strange feeling took root in my brain. It felt like a thousand spider eggs had hatched inside my brain. My bad habits were blossoming into uncontrollable addictions. This feeling was proof of an insistent needfulness. I pressed the back of my hand against my eye to stop the throbbing. My eye felt like it might pop.

"You look tired," she stated.

"I feel like I'm being evicted from my childhood. Also, the nightmares of what the people are doing in my bed are disturbing," I told her.

I lowered my hand and peered through narrowed eyes. Brilliant white streaks sailed across my field of vision like comets, cutting through the night sky. It was impossible to make out anything else. My eyes felt wet and glossy. I wasn't crying, though.

"You don't know the whole story," she began. "Your mom lost her job. Her father has been giving her cash since the divorce. He put a down payment on the trailer. The deal was finalized last week! Your mom has bought new furniture and moved it in already."

CHAPTER 22

Dark clouds made the hour of the autumn day feel later. One at a time, raindrops tumbled down from the sky. I left the house feeling troubled, driving toward the city of Wilmington. The weather grew worse as I came within a closer proximity of my destination.

Weedeater mentioned a certain bar his motorcycle club drank at with regularity. My search was hampered by the foul weather. The downpour of rain outpaced the windshield wipers. The city streets appeared dark and gloomy. It would be a falsehood to state that the bar was found without aid.

I stopped at a gas station to refuel my car. It almost ran out of gas, circling the city. I must have driven past the dive bar three or four times. The cashier gave precise directions.

The parking lot was empty except for my car. It sat long enough for the cool damp air to seep inside. Lightning raced across the sky in beautiful and terrifying flashes. The din of thunder rattled across my car windshield.

Heavy rain never lasted very long in a small state like Delaware. A second vehicle entered the parking lot after the downpour ended. A woman with long red hair parked her vehicle behind the bar. After a while, she unlocked the doors. The woman tending bar was not one to suffer fools.

"Nothing to minors," she stated.

"I have ID," I answered.

She didn't return the license into my hand—just slapped it down on the wooden bar. I jammed my license inside my wallet. Then I removed a ten-dollar bill and placed it on the bar.

"In a hurry to start day drinking?" She asked.

"I need someone to help me locate a friend of mine," I said.

"You want to take care of business first? I'm here to serve drinks."

"Grand Marnier neat with a Miller Light chaser."

"Got it on tap. Draft, okay?"

"Yeah, okay."

Actually, rubbing alcohol would have sufficed to satisfy my craving. I couldn't hold the small glass of liquor study. I felt like the last fall leaf hanging onto a branch with all my might. The first shot of liquor burned inside my chest. The draft beer went down like a cool refreshing breeze.

The bartender studied me with sensitive eyes. My body felt tense for a different reason. She was attractive in a rough-hewn manner. The smile on her face felt contagious. She hunched over, leaning on the bar for support.

"I'm Robin," she revealed.

"You keep that," I urged.

I slid the ten-dollar bill closer to her. Then I placed a twenty on top of the ten. She left the money on the bar. One thing was evident; we proceeded according to her rules. I was eager to continue our conversation.

"Do you know what happened to the bouncer that worked here?" I asked.

"Different guys watch the bar door every weekend," she replied.

"He belongs to a local motorcycle club," I said.

Robin didn't respond to my statement. She replaced the empty glasses with fresh drinks. Next, she took the money and entered the transaction into the register.

"You gonna be okay for a minute? I've got some prep to take care of," she said.

She disappeared from sight, and I studied the sparse decor. The bar was decorated in a Western saloon motif. I selected a Bon Jovi song on the jukebox. He sang about cowboys and steel horses over a cool guitar riff.

I was drunk before another patron entered the bar. Half an hour later, there weren't many empty seats. Then the roar of motorcycle engines resonated from the parking lot. The noise filled the bar with a nervous energy.

The bikers entered the bar and walked toward a table that was already occupied by patrons. Those patrons relinquished their seats. I observed the motorcycle club insignia. It was the same insignia Weedeater had sewn on his jacket.

I needed to use the restroom. My head spun and I was unsteady on my feet. I only half-pissed in the urinal. The rest ended up on the floor or splashed back on me.

I returned to find someone had taken my seat. My lowered inhibitions gave me the courage to approach the bikers. "Do any of you know how I can find Weedeater?" I asked.

"How about a Hedge Trimmer or a Lawn Mower?" A biker joked.

"No."

I leaned on the table and spoke in a whisper. "He's in your gang."

"You know who I haven't seen in a while? Your mom," the biker added.

I walked away as their laughter rang out in a series of full rich tones. Robin observed my dejected conduct. She wrote something on the back of a beer coaster. It was presented to me upon my arrival at the bar.

"What's this?" I inquired.

"Call that number. You'll find what you're looking for," she replied.

"Can I get another round?"

"No. You need to be sober enough to drive."

She gave me a cold glare. The whole situation made me feel impatient. My muscles felt like wire cables on a tension bridge. My entire body shook like a homeless wino in winter. There was an acrid taste in the back of my throat. I exited the bar with an unsteady gait.

The raucous activity inside the bar became a monotonous hum inside my head. My level of intoxication was apparent as I struggled to find a home for the key to my car door. Someone seized me from behind as I fumbled with the lock and the key. Another person helped this powerful individual carry me to a secluded area behind the bar.

They placed me down on the ground with considerate handling. Then the powerful individual placed a large boot on my crotch. He applied a downward pressure marked with an intense pain that forced my compliance. "Where are you off to in such a hurry?" He asked.

The bikers from the bar surrounded me like a horde of modern-day Vikings. They looked amused by the situation.

I had nothing to answer their wry grins. My struggle to remove the large boot was unsuccessful.

"Weedeater is in the county jail," a biker said.

A few days later, I sped toward the county jail. Traffic on the northbound lanes of I-95 was sparse. Rock music blared on the radio. I thought it would be prudent to arrive early for the scheduled visit.

A fence topped with razor wire surrounded the jail in all directions. I waited outside the only entrance for guards to examine my vehicle. A loud impact on the window made me jump. I lowered the window faster than normal. There was an increase in my heart rate. As I answered questions in a high-pitched voice. A guard waved for the gates to open, afterwards.

Inmate HB 8964, as he was known to the judicial system, sat alone in a large room crowded with square tables. Brian Walker was his real name. He hadn't gone to trial yet. I began the visit with an embrace. He didn't reciprocate too much. Cuffs and shackles remained on during the brief visit.

We talked in low voices. I described how his fellow bikers had humiliated me. A grin spread across his face while the story unfolded. He expressed his concern about my level of involvement. I could hear the tension in his voice. He lifted his handcuffed wrists as a gesture to emphasize his point.

A guard appeared and escorted him out. I told him to expect a letter from me soon. I couldn't stand the thought of losing my friend in the event of a long prison sentence. It should have been a greater deterrent.

In fact, I contacted a potential new source of drugs following my visit to the jail. I was nervous about meeting a new dealer, nervous I might be turned down, or have my money stolen. My personal safety was another concern.

Addiction influenced my thought and behavior, told me everything I needed to hear. It felt like drugs were taking me on a journey of self-discovery. This was a lie. They were leading me away from my best self. Only time would reveal this fact, however.

Later that night, I arrived at Ripe Tomatoes. This was going to be a big night. It would be the first night without the owner's supervision. Ryan had decided to give me a chance. I didn't receive a warm welcome from him or the other employees.

Six o'clock in the evening, the phones were flooded with calls from college students. Students overran Main Street. Wild parties had begun all over campus. The campus was a giant playground for young adults. I experienced the debauchery firsthand.

My first delivery was to a dorm. A student waited for his delivery in the open doorway. He stumbled against the entrance, reaching inside his pocket for money. A prideful smile spread across his face after the payment was in my hand.

Suddenly, he hunched over in the hallway. A fountain of foam and stomach bile spewed from his mouth. A roar of laughter came from his companions inside the room. I asked the nearest person in the room to carry the pizza boxes. Someone took the boxes and the door swung closed in my face. My pants and shoes were flecked with the vomit.

A large delivery awaited me at the pizzeria. The address belonged to a fraternity house. I was unfamiliar with that area of campus. The streets were lined with vehicles. It was impossible to find a parking spot near the house. So I was forced to carry the large order from a block away.

The location was overrun with students intoxicated beyond typical moral sense. They relieved me of my heavy burden. No one offered to pay for the food, though. I began a search of the premises for someone to provide payment.

The fraternity house was crowded beyond its capacity. Drinks were sloshed upon me. I circulated the house for quite some time. Time to make additional deliveries slipped away.

Eventually, I navigated a path into the backyard. The backyard was less crowded. One young man was passed out on a lawn chair.

I presumed he would have a wallet on his person. So I conducted a search of his pockets. His wallet contained a large sum of money. I stuffed the money into my pocket. The wallet was left in a very noticeable place. It was my intention to leave with the money.

Retracing my steps, I navigated the narrow passages between bodies inside the house. A couple of familiar faces caught my attention. I looked across the room at Linda and Toni. Linda noticed my delivery outfit. Her lips stretched into a delighted sneer. She clutched Toni's arm, forcing Toni to remain at her side. I strode toward the door without further hesitation.

I walked at a rapid pace until the house was almost out of sight. Then I turned to study the house, expecting Toni to emerge. She did not follow me, however. My thoughts were thrown into disarray.

When the mental fog cleared, I was no closer to finding my car. I lost my bearings in the unfamiliar surroundings. The biting cold sent a chill down my spine. I made the decision to end the search for my car. The pizzeria was less than a mile away. A dim light illuminated the inside. There was only one car left in the dark parking lot. I approached the large window and gave it a light pounding with the side of my fist. Ryan emerged from the office. He peered out into the shadows of the parking lot. Then he opened the door to allow me entrance into the shop.

"What happened to you?" He asked.

"I lost my car," I replied.

"That's a first," he said.

"Give me your payment. So I can close out the receipts," he urged.

By the time I had arrived at the pizzeria, it was around 2:00 a.m. The other drivers had finished cleaning before they left. I studied their handiwork and searched for something to keep me occupied while Ryan completed his tally. Something unexpected happened, however.

At first, I doubted my own senses. The smell of marijuana permeated the pizzeria. I thought it may have been something in the oven. So I inspected the oven. My suspicion was incorrect.

Next, I noticed plumes of smoke pouring out of the office. Ryan sat inside the office with a wide grin. He chuckled at the dumbfounded expression on my face.

"I'd offer you some, but you reek of alcohol and vomit. Have you been drinking?" He said.

"No, it's been an interesting night. A customer got sick on me. People spilled drinks all over me." I explained.

"What happened to your car?"

"I lost my bearings at the fraternity."

"It's over by the Row?"

"Greek Row."

"Yeah. You're not getting into my car like that, though. Do you have boxers on?"

"Yeah."

"Put your clothes in a garbage bag. I don't want that stench contaminating my car."

The search for my car didn't take very long. Traffic had lessened throughout the early morning hours. Ryan was very familiar with the area. He drove with a narrow gap in his window. The cold air turned my exposed skin to goose flesh.

"That looks like your car up ahead," he announced.

"Yeah. That's it," I replied.

I watched Ryan drive away through the front windshield of my car. Then I counted my earnings. The amount was nowhere near enough to pay my debt of student loans.

EPILOGUE

There were no Gothic buildings with giant columns, no sports stadium, no manicured courtyards, and no sprawling campus regarding the community college. Del Tech had one main campus. The largest building lacked enough character to give a vivid representation in words. My eyes ran up and down the front of the building from the huge parking lot. A sigh escaped my lips.

I fell in step with the other students, funneling toward the entrance. Everyone glanced around with obvious expectation. My stomach felt queasy from the paroxysm of nerves. I pressed forward, walking parallel with a stranger.

Finally, I traversed the spacious lot and entered through a red brick facade. The building was bustling inside as well. Many students flocked to the school store to make last-minute purchases. Others went to a small food court for coffee or something to eat. I navigated the complex at a rapid pace and finding my first class on the second floor.

The instructor didn't acknowledge my entrance into the classroom. He lectured through the entire class period. There was a lot of material to get through in just one semester. I took plenty of notes seated at the back of the class. My notes included everything the instructor wrote on the board and a few remarks he made.

In addition, on the opposite page, I wrote down notes about everyone in the class. My focus was on finding the perfect candidate for a new study group. It was near impossible to gauge their intelligence. The laundry list of peculiar habits did not suggest my classmates were intellectual savants, however.

Fingers were gnawed. Pencils were tapped on various surfaces. Hair was manipulated. Even I found my knee bounced in an involuntary manner.

An Asian male presented the most interesting behavior. His hands moved as though he was playing a piano. He pressed down on the surface of the desk hard enough to squeeze the blood out of the capillaries in his fingertips. I noticed his nail beds turn white from the pressure.

There was a fellow student who caught my attention in the second class. She was a plain-looking young woman. Her eyes were brown, but they weren't totally artless. They were large and spoke of an innocence, in part due to her brief life. Her hair was straight and a remarkable brown color like maple syrup. I took notice of a repeated motion. She tucked her hair behind her ears many times.

The second instructor began to lecture in a soft soothing voice. Notes were taken in the same manner as they were in the first class. The instructor was very strategic. She stayed on topic and never once mentioned any personal references to illustrate a point.

Eventually, the first day of classes came to an end. I left the classroom, feeling relieved to be free from the parasitic element of learning. It was not just a matter of the material teachers provided; it was also what students were able to do with it. New material complicated our clashes with preliminary thinking. It was difficult to be open to opinions that run counter to our own initial ones.

I walked toward the exit with a flyer in my hand. The bottom edge of the paper was fringed. My pager number was on each separate piece. I found a bulletin board just outside the school store. This was where the flyer for my study group could gather public interest. Or not. In fact, I don't believe it ever piqued anyone's interest.

Later, I met Toni at a bar and restaurant on her campus. Deer Park was located on the southwest corner of Main Street. It was normal for students to pack the place. Toni was waiting alone in a booth. She sat with one arm propped on the table, her face rested on the back of her hand. The look on her face was serene.

I touched her shoulder and leaned in for a quick kiss. We decided to have an early supper. We held hands for a long time until our food arrived. We were both a little quiet.

After supper and a few drinks, we went to her dorm room. The first thing I did was check for Linda. No one was there except the two of us.

"So what's the plan?" I asked.

"You're going to watch me study for a while. Then you're going to leave. How does that sound?" She replied.

"Doesn't the excitement on my face say it all?" I equipped.

We sat on the edge of her bed and enjoyed some casual flirtation. She made circles around my ear with her index finger. It felt like all the stress and tension from earlier was leaving my body.

"I left a flyer for a new study group on a bulletin board at school," I mentioned.

"Why not keep it the two of us?" She asked.

"We don't have the same material to study."

"So you want to meet with a bunch of strangers to get stoned and study?"

"It worked in high school."

The End